AN ORBITING
DILEMMA

AN ORBITING DILEMMA

BRETT WORTHAM

An orbiting Dilemma
Copyright © 2019 by Brett Wortham. All rights reserved.

No part of this publication may be reproduced, stored in a retrieval system or transmitted in any way by any means, electronic, mechanical, photocopy, recording or otherwise without the prior permission of the author except as provided by USA copyright law.

This novel is a work of fiction. Names, descriptions, entities, and incidents included in the story are products of the author's imagination. Any resemblance to actual persons, events, and entities is entirely coincidental.

The opinions expressed by the author are not necessarily those of URLink Print and Media.

1603 Capitol Ave., Suite 310 Cheyenne, Wyoming USA 82001
1-888-980-6523 | admin@urlinkpublishing.com

URLink Print and Media is committed to excellence in the publishing industry.

Book design copyright © 2019 by URLink Print and Media. All rights reserved.

Published in the United States of America

ISBN 978-1-64367-896-2 (Paperback)
ISBN 978-1-64367-895-5 (Digital)

19.09.19

A big dear thanks to my loving and supportive family and also the Willox family and my beloved Aunt Barbra Dolan for granting me the first monies to get this dang thing published in the first place! And singularly by the grace of God too!

A man was found running in a hilly forest for his life from a mixture mob of all sorts of aliens and people. All of them were yelling angrily as they ran to catch this poor fellow. Some were even carrying pitchforks and torches. This unfortunate cuss was running with a stunningly beautiful blond woman in his arms. This woman was dressed as a bride and had the look of pure rapture and contentment on her face as she stared affectionately into the face of the man who was carrying her.

Once the man rounded a corner of the trail path, he thought things couldn't possibly get any worse than they were now. As if on cue a huge angry looking two-legged reverse kneed mechanical big laser gunned war machine walker rumbled out of the forest snapping trees coming up right after him joining the mob in the chase pointing its blasters at him and the girl.

"Aww come OONNN!!!" yelled the man as soon as he saw the TW4 join in the pursuit. He was breathing heavily now with that astonishingly beautiful blond woman in his arms wondering how in the worlds he got into this mess. It probably started right after his brunch date with his girlfriend he thought. Now we turn back the clock to an earlier time.

We start this story by focusing our attention on a moon world named Drylon 3. A big colony was set up on this moon because of all the precious minerals and gases that were found on Drylon the gas giant planet itself. This planet/moon became a colony so that miners who go to the dangerous environment of Drylon itself wouldn't be too far away from their families. For Drylon's environment was very inhospitable to most life forms. The colony flourished as workers came to live in it bringing slews of businessmen and entrepreneurs looking to make their fortunes at this highly productive and successful colony not even one hundred and eleven years old yet.

A young man parked his old but still usable hover car in a spot he had been using over these past months. For quite a few months he had been coming here with his girlfriend once he found out she loved this view of the city. He got out and grabbed all the picnic items he chose for this little spree putting them to the side by his hover car. Once done with that he stood there staring at the pile of paraphernalia he had piled up. He scratched his brown-haired head wondering how he was going to get all that up the hill.

"Need any help carrying all that stuff Yurri?" a blond young woman asked the young man.

"Nah Janice I can get it," he said waving to his girlfriend. "You just take the food basket up there and find a spot you like with a good view." It was Yurri Banx's day off and he planned to spend it with a girl that surprisingly approved of being his girlfriend.

"Alright then." She gave him a smile whisking bright yellow blond bangs off her face carrying the food basket. As she walked away Yurri couldn't help but ogle her perfect beautiful and very shapely form wondering how he had ever landed such a catch. He had only asked her out on a dare from one of his fellow coworkers at the restaurant where he worked.

Janice had on a more modest dress today. It was a one-piece brown and blue dress with a knee length divided skirt with the blue parts on top becoming browner as it got lower.

It had the effect of accentuating all her curves more though it did cover her up to her neck. She, of course, had her marvelous purse with her. It was plain with various shades of browns and reds and blues. She seemed to be able to fit almost anything into it from what Yurri's seen her pull out of it so far. It was decorated in such a way that it would make a good accessory with almost any type of clothing she wore. She also wore some decorations in her hair. Since meeting her she has always had that same type of hair decoration on. It was surprisingly bland and bulky to be seen on a girl like Janice. She usually wore her blond hair untied long brushing over her shoulders and back with that hair decoration weaved on just to accentuate her look and keep her hair manageable. This girl also had on a pair of stylish short top outdoor boots too. They were colorful with playful patterns around these stylish yet serviceable short boots that could easily blend into multiple grass and ground type colors while not being an eye sore as well.

 She was halfway up the hill by the time Yurri came to himself from pondering his good fortune shaking his head. He frowned at the pile of picnic gear wondering how he would carry it all. He had the bad habit of always over preparing for things. He had even brought a humungous picnic umbrella. He looked up the short but steep climb of the hill rethinking on whether or not to bring that with him. The young man decided to leave the umbrella in the hover car and carefully wrapped up all other picnic items in the picnic blanket his girlfriend and him would be lying on while having their meal.

 Yurri was about as average as a person could get but still, he thought he had a decent figure for carrying heavy things. With brown hair and brown eyes there was nothing overly identifying about his looks. He could easily get lost in a crowd. Usually he wore clothing that had extra pockets in them and habitually carried an odd assortment of random items he generally found a use for at odd times. His clothes were loose, a dull brown on his shirt, with black pants, and they had a comfortable fit on him. The shoes on this young man wore were dark brown sturdy but worn lace up work shoes.

The young man slung the picnic bag over his shoulder and made the short but steep trip up the hill. He found his girlfriend in a clearing by a grove of trees; it was those red singing trees. The leaves of this peculiar plant were shaped in a way that they made an odd musical whistling sound when the wind blew through them. There was a crap load of mythological stories about this very tree also, but the young man never really listened to much history about this planet since he got here a couple years ago. He considered it weird that these types of trees had some mythological lore to them at all. This planet didn't have its own residential sentient species so how could they get their own mythological stories? This planet wasn't that old with people living on it.

Another one of Yurri's bad habits was not taking in any information about the place he was currently living at right now. It took him years to get comfortable with a new place before he started to know how to get around properly. At first, he thought he would be here for only a couple months while his parents dealt with a problem at home, but things didn't seem to be getting settled back there so he was stuck here.

As he came to the top of the hill, with picnic items slung over his shoulder, he saw his girlfriend frolicking, playing, and singing with some of the local fauna of this area. Birds were tweeting in tune with the sad song of a forced and arranged marriage, an unwanted marriage apparently, that Janice was singing about. As she was singing some squirrel type rodents were dancing in step with her. Yurri only shook his head when he saw this. He found it wasn't worth the energy to be surprised around this girl anymore. If a girl this beautiful, with a few exceptionally weird quirks, wanted to date a remarkably normal guy like him who was he to make a fuss over something as minor as being able to communicate with animals? No matter how creepy that was...

"Hey Jan, where do you want to set this up?" he called out. His girlfriend's small animal friends scattered at his shout.

"Why don't we settle down over where we last had this picnic of ours?" Janice said pointing while adjusting her clothes and hair picking up her purse and their picnic basket.

She picked a spot on top of the hill they were on that had a spectacular view of the city placing their basket on the ground. The young man quickly unpacked his burden and laid it all out almost methodically. Yurri was cheap — *Who could blame him for the meager salary he made?*— and they had done this same thing multiple times. Janice never complained though. Probably because his family had some connections here on this planet and he could get them low priced or free tickets too to many of the cultural events on this planet. Janice had a kind of fetish for anything that was labeled as art or an innovating cultural event. Especially when it involved some sort of clothing or hair style.

After having set up on a spot that Janice seemed to favor over these past couple of months, they opened up their picnic basket and ate while chatting after a quick prayer of thanks to the same gods they both worship. "Did you hear?" Janice asked while lying on her side with the food she was eating on a cloth napkin. "Master Highquasar just opened up a new branch at his Jai Academy on Xevim 3!" She smiled as she nibbled on her breakfast sandwich. "They are now enlisting people to train there as young as preteens!" Apparently, she had this little obsession about the mysterious order of the Archai Yirujie. Yurri didn't mind though. He only looked into her eyes occasionally nodding into compliance with what she was talking about. She continued by telling Yurri that she would just die if it were found out she could train to be a Jai too. Their conversation continued in the like manner.

"Did you know that the power they use is called the Archai?" she giggled putting down her breakfast sandwich looking at him grinning like she just figured out a hilarious joke that had escaped her before. "The Archai power or the energy of it all comes from living things. Including planets." She nodded her head seriously at him. "Life's energy basically. It allows all of us to exist!" Jan giggled and smiled while she nibbled some more off her sandwich. "Mmm, these sandwiches you made are so good! What type of berry thing did you say the jam was made out of again?"

"Sea water fruits I think," Yurri said searching his memory for the name. He had pilfered this jam from his restaurant boss's private stash of exotic food. "I got it off the extra stock my boss had stashed away. Can't remember what planet it comes from though. Maybe one of the vastly ocean planets I think," he said crunching on some of the chips he brought.

"Well it is yummy!" she said while munching on her sandwich some more. After the third chomp she paused her chewing looking lost. She swallowed hard gasping "What was I talking about again?" She ended that question with a finger on her lip looking puzzled/cute at the young man.

"The Archai Yirujie and the meaning of their name I think," Yurri said trying to be helpful. He enjoyed it when she was puzzled and gave him that look.

"Oh yeah!" she said cat pawing his shoulder. "Silly of me to forget!" She put down her food breathing in. "The name Archai Yirujie has some certain symbolism to it. Though…" she paused looking glum. "Most of that meaning and symbolism of that name was lost in well over thirty years ago during the Jai purge thanks to that meanie ol' Kaiser Khan Yach and his army of druggies he sent to kill the vast majority of them and any of their historical records." She pouted.

Indeed, the old Kaiser Yach had used trickery and treachery to squeeze himself into positions of power in the old United Systems government. After the Kaiser's death the vast majority of solar systems reset and implemented well known and smaller government attributes to their respective governments again. The systems in the universe became stable again after that.

"I think it's lucky that Master Jim Highquasar was part of a family that was Archai Yirujie that didn't follow the old dictates of their order. Did you know that the Jai of old didn't allow each other to get married and have children? Of course that old order was dying out if you didn't let any of your members get married!" Janice put a hand to her face to partly hide her grimace.

Yup... Yurri had heard her talk about this dozens of times before but he didn't mind. It was basic history. Well basic with how Yurri was raised anyways. It was cute the way she acted when telling him this story. And she also couldn't hide her excitement when she told him that the new Jai could finally marry. He supposed she would get really cozy really quickly with any young Jai man she met. This didn't bug Yurri though. It really didn't. He already knew and accepted that Janice was out of his league. It was simply fun to be around this quirky beautiful girl and he would enjoy as much time of it as he could and let the future settle itself out.

"Something about letting themselves get too attached to people and things... leading them to feel hatred and anger or something. So they lived a boring celibate life never getting those things that actually make life worth living!" she bit her left knuckle looking upset. Yurri patted her shoulder nodding his head. She smiled a thank you at him and continued. "So yes, it was lucky that Master Jim's family weren't following those old Jai rules. Allowing Master Jim to be born and grow up learning from his dad how to be a Jai. Although Jim's grandfather, Phil I think his name was, died trying to keep his family's secret safe. I think Phil died just before Benjimyn, one of his older sons, fell to a darker path."

"A darker path than what?" Yurri asked her, knowing she enjoyed telling him the whole back story to this history.

She gave him a grin thanking him for playing along. He may have earned a little more snuggle time tonight when they go to the live theaters. She sat herself up more erect with her legs modestly bent to her side sitting on them. She breathed in, "The Archai Yirujie is an ancient order of skilled warrior protectors with special powers. They label themselves as Stellar Cavaliers or a special type of space knight, though I don't know why they don't just call themselves that. Copy write infringements I think." Yurri shrugged agreeing with her. She took another bite out of her sandwich giving a complimenting mmm sound after she swallowed. After taking a little sip from her water bottle, she continued. "The old Jai kept peace and order throughout the whole galaxy while the old interspatial government was going on, but it got too big for its britches and evil people crept in and took it over. Because the old Jai order was opposed to all the corruption that was going on, they used some genocidal techniques to eliminate the vast majority of the Jai order. Master Jim Highquasar's uncle Benjimyn, one of Phil's sons, was tricked by the evil Kaiser Khan into tracking down and killing the old Jai order. Phil had helped sneak his son into the Archai Yirujie order cuz Benji wanted to do good but that zeal to do good had a sad ending..." Jan clasped her hands with a sad look on her face. "The old Kaiser made Benjimyn think his secret wife was killed by the old Jai sect when in fact the evil old Kaiser secretly killed her himself and shifted the blame.

Old Benji even believed they killed his entire family. But in fact, Dan, Master Jim's dad, hid himself, Master Jim, Jim's sisters and their families, and all his family members away from all the bad things that were happening in the galaxy by moving them to the outer rims. I think Dan hid his entire family in a weird Archai disruption field or something so that the evil Khan couldn't find them right away. Don't really know the specifics on that one." She wiped her face with a napkin.

"So how did Master Jim kill the evil Khan in the end?" Yurri asked smiling knowing what this question would bring.

"Oh, now that is a mistake most people make!" she said wagging a finger, from the hand that was holding her napkin, in his face. "You'd think Master Jim did it himself, seeing that he founded the new Archai Yirujie Academy. Well it was actually Master Jim's uncle that killed the evil Kaiser, old Benji. A band of the rebel faction got into the Kahn's moon/palace and were making as much noise as they could. To distract the Khan from a small team of specialists which consisted of Master Jim, his father Dan, with a couple of Jim's cousins and brothers, and a few stalwart fellows too. They thought they could overpower the evil Kaiser Khan by the sheer number of Archai users. Here let me show you."

Putting her napkin down she reached into her marvelous purse and after fumbling around in it a minute she brought out her rectangular shaped Trans Tablet, a device that could do many things for its user. "Here," she said turning it on. Its flat screen turned on showing several of options she could choose to do. She tapped her picture gallery and maximized the picture she chose turning it into a projected holo image as she laid it down in front of her. "There," she said pointing to a red headed stout sharp featured faced young man among a group of people in old style clothes. "That is younger Master Jim Highquasar." She smiled affectionately at the image.

"He's much older now though. He is also married with quite a few children too," she said glumly. "But, as I was saying, he wasn't the one who took down the evil Kaiser. That was old Benji. Old Benjimyn was fighting his younger brother Dan using his dark Dawn Sword, or Lumin Blade, or Lumin Brand, or Bright Spar... You know... the Jai aren't very clear on what the official name of what their special weapons are. Though I do think they generally call um luminblades." She shrugs happily not understanding and continued with her story. "Anyways Benji recognizes his brother's fighting style and starts asking him questions. I guess he had a hard time recognizing his younger brother after not seeing him for so long and believing him dead too."

After taking another small sip from her water bottle Jan paused looking like she was remembering something. "Oh yeah!" she exclaimed clapping her hands. "I forgot to put in the premise to this big fight! You'd think I was a blond or something." she said winking at Yurri smiling at her own stereo type. "The whole premise behind this big fight was in the reactor core of the Kahn's moon/palace. Apparently evil old Yach had been planning for an intrusion like this. So when the Highquasar family and company entered the throne room and were about to take the Kaiser out the floor beneath them fell away dropping them all into the big reactor core. The family and company landed in an area full of men who had taken the Izo drug."

"You remember the Izo drug right Yurri?" She looked up at him expectantly. When he nodded, she gave him a wonderful smile and continued on. "The Izo drug is also exceptionally rare, massively expensive, and an extremely lethal drug. This drug is outlawed in practically every system because it's so dangerous. Not even the black market carries much of it. Guess it kills their customers too quickly to make it worth it." She shrugged. "When people take it, their very skin starts turning black literally rotting away as they live. The longest I've ever heard of someone living from this was about two days. A galaxy record. The only reason anyone takes this poison is because it gives them Jai powers and makes them much stronger. But after a couple hours or so a persons' body starts to go into uncontrollable and horribly painful convolutions if they can't control it. But as anyone knows already no matter how much of this drug someone takes a true Archai user will have the advantage considering that the true person had already received much training with the usage of it before. So all these druggies were keeping our Jai family and friends busy while Benjimyn and his brother Dan fought fighting each other with their luminblades. Benji starts asking his brother questions but when it looks like Ben is having a change of heart the evil old Kaiser Kahn unleashes a wicked blast of red lightning at Jim, Dan's son."

"AAACHOO!!" Janice's explanation was interrupted by an enormous sneeze coming abruptly from her nose. Yurri handed her one of his clean unused handkerchiefs, with a few worn slightly torn edges, which she used to lightly blow out her nose some more and clean her face. When done she tried to give it back but Yurri waved her off telling her to keep it for now. She wrapped it up and stuck it in her purse for later use. "Anyways, as I was saying, Dan saw that his son was in trouble, so he broke off from his fight with his brother and intercepted the bolt with his luminblade and faced off with the evil Kaiser one on one. I hear it was a horrific fight with all the Archai users around and this amazing fight between two seasoned Archai users. But sadly, Dan wasn't a match for the evil old Kaiser Kahn and was thoroughly struck down by his wicked red lightning. This enraged Jim and he struck out at the Kahn. Ben stood there stunned as he saw his younger brother die in front of eyes blasted away to ashes. I believe he was still in shock finding out his family still lived. Seeing his younger brother die suddenly in front of his eyes made Benjimyn snap out of the funk he had been in for years. Because the Kahn was busy fighting Jim, he didn't see the immensely saddened and enraged Ben rush him from behind." Jan sniffed wiping her eyes. Looking up to Yurri with a sad smile she said, "Old Benji bull rushed the Kaiser Kahn and himself into a fiery blue plasma field that had been broken out by all the intense fighting going on in that big reactor core room." Jan sniffed again wiping her eyes. She looked up to Yurri with a sad yet happy look on her face. "Old Benji did the trick. As soon as those druggies saw their Kaiser go down none of them wanted to see how this ended considering the fact that they all faced a gruesome and painful deaths they all immediately took their own lives. I won't go into the details there." She frowned. "From what I've heard it was messy."

She took another small bite of her sandwich and immediately perked up after swallowing. "So yes!" she said abruptly slapping her hands on her knees. "Because the core took a big hit from both the enraged Benjimyn and the red lightning blasting Kaiser Kahn it was about to explode! All of our heroes made a mad dash and barely escaped the explosion." Janice grinned at the telling of the exciting getaway. "Nowadays Master Jim Highquasar leads the new Archai Yirujie academy on Xevim 3, another moon/planet not much unlike the one we're on right now." She smiled breathing in and sampled some chips from the same bag that Yurri was eating from.

"So, we know this history of the new Jai academy, but one thing still confuses me a little bit," Yurri said as he held out the chip bag for her. "Why is their nickname Jai instead of Jie? You know… How it's spelled in Yirujie… The last three letters of Yirujie. I think logically it should be Jie instead of

Jai," Yurri said awkwardly seeing that he was losing her in his reasoning.

Janice gave him one of her cute confused looks and tapped her lip. She shrugged it off. "I don't really understand your complaint here Yurri. A Jai is still a Jie no matter how you spell them." She smirked at him entertained by his odd thoughts. "So yes, what I just figured out was that their full title is Archai Yirujie and Archai is the name of their power! So, the name of their power is in their full title! That just dawned on me!" She lightly slapped her forehead smiling at Yurri. "Oh, and also from some sources it is believed that Yirujie anciently means 'wielder of' or something along those lines. So, in that translation their name means 'Wielders of Archai'!" She finished with splaying out her hands excitedly finishing off her show.

"Well heck. All I really know about the Jai is that they intimidate me," he admitted shrugging with a quirked weak smile. Yurri also didn't mind learning more about the Jai, which made him nervous, as long as he could enjoy looking into her stunning azure eyes and see her smile.

"The Jai of old were very secretive and for a while everybody thought they were extinct. You're only uncomfortable with them because their order, fairly renewed or new, is mainly unknown to you and everybody else silly. I usually get the same way when entering a new shopping mall I don't know. Where are the bathrooms? Where is the cafeteria? And most important of all where do they keep their shoe stores?! This one time I almost went into hysterical fits because I thought I lost my precious purse. My Daddy made this for me, so I could never part from it," she said while affectionately stroking her monstrous purse. Yurri thought you could stuff a small adult body in there if you tucked it in just right. "After some help from an attendant I finally found it in a grocery bag I had tucked it in earlier." She winked and stuck her tongue out at him, "Silly of me to forget something like that."

Indeed, it was. Just what type of mall does she go to where they have bags big enough for a monster purse like hers? Yurri merely shook his head and chuckled politely. Behavior like this from her doesn't surprise him anymore. From the first time he met her she has acted as if she were trying to get used to being a blond, really weird… because she seemed to be a natural blond anyways. With all the quirky and stereotypical behaviors that came along with it. Yurri had to admit that this type of behavior was quite cute and endearing.

Their conversation halted abruptly when both started hearing a high light rumble coming from over a taller part of the hill. They both stood up trying to discern what was making that foreboding sound. As they stared alerted watching the top of the hill a large gray armored man jetted over the hill coming towards them. When only a dozen yards away he lunged down slamming to the ground making Yurri's teeth chatter from the impact. After standing up properly from that big landing the ominous man glared knives at Yurri while giving Jan a grizzled smile. "Jan! I've finally found you after months of searching! Why did you hide yourself from me?" the man said while moving towards the couple. "You know I would personally hand you the head of anyone that got on your bad side," he said while spreading his hands out. This man had a buzz cut but even with a buzz cut his smokey brown hair looked somehow unkempt.

Jan turned white while grabbing her cheeks like she does when she's baffled or upset. She looked to Yurri as if he might help her with this somehow. But she drew her look away from her boyfriend, squared her shoulders, and missiled harpoons at the intruder with the glare she gave him. "Ron, I left you because I want a man who can feel compassion for others and help people out of the goodness of his heart, not to charge them for your help afterwards." Janice turned away with a tear running down her cheek. "Like how you refused to help that poor old woman fight off that huge carnivorous Nixdon bear."

The armored man, Ron, gave her a look that was exasperated and said she should know better. "That old woman did just fine by herself. She did win that fight in the end. I heard she has forty-two grandchildren," Ron rationalized. "She didn't need my help after all. You should have seen the state the bear was in afterwards. I've never seen a body cast that big before."

Janice glared again at Ron. "She lost the bottom half of her left leg!" she snapped fiercely at him. "She wouldn't have had to go through all that pain and suffering if you had helped out of the goodness of your heart!"

"I'm a bounty hunter Jan." Ron took a step toward Janice and Yurri. Janice stepped back pulling Yurri along with her. "This is the way I've chosen to live my life. The first time I met you it didn't seem to bother you much." He gave her an exasperated and impatient look. "Ever since that first date we went on you've been on my mind constantly. Why can't you return my affections like you should?"

Janice gave Ron a surprisingly sharp look again and sniffed loudly. "That first date was only because I felt sorry for you." Ron started to interject but Janice plowed over him. "You were doing a job on Kineekon working for a politician to hunt down the people that kidnapped his daughter."

"I remember that. That guy paid me pretty well."

Janice looked a little flustered at being interrupted but she went on telling the story without commenting on this rude injection. "After hearing what you did on Kineekon with you saving that poor little girl made me feel pity for you, so I said yes."

"You did have me ask you about twenty times before you said yes or even looked at me," Ron injected again.

"That is not the topic of this conversation!" Janice's face and hair, Yurri thought that the lighting did this for the hair, reddened a little bit. "I found you were a sad little man that couldn't get a friend if you didn't bully them first! The dates we went on were out of pure pity which I don't think you deserve right now!" Janice sharply turned away from Ron flipping her ever reddening -*it must be the lighting*- long hair over her shoulder.

She wouldn't look at him anymore or affirm that he was even there. After a couple more attempts of trying to get her attention, which didn't work, Ron sighed and glared at Yurri puffing out his chest. "The only way I can see to win back your heart is to duel your Jai boyfriend, kill him, and buy you that gemlon ruby dress you always wanted."

This was getting way too out of hand. Yurri had to think quickly. "Hey!" he shouted, pointing randomly to some dense foliage. "Isn't that Draxus Lenox, who has a seven hundred million credit bounty on his head?"

Ron turned his head to look where Yurri had been pointing. "Where?" he asked like the idiot he was.

"Come on, let's run, Jan!" Yurri grabbed Janice by the arm and ran into the woods while Ron still searched for the many million credit bounty man that Yurri had made up.

As they ran through the forest, they could hear Ron scream, "You goober! Tell me where that seven hundred million credit man is, or I'll do some very unpleasant things to your reproductive organs!"

Yurri and Janice ran into the more forested area of the park. This large park made it easy to hide from that crazy bounty hunter. As they ran, they got lost. After a long while of running aimlessly Janice pulled herself away from Yurri, fell against a tree, and gasped for breath. "I didn't know you were a Jai, Yurri," she said, between pants, with a surprised look on her face.

"Neither did I," admitted a still gasping Yurri. "Uhh," he rethought what he just said. He might never get another chance to get to know a gal like Janice again, "I mean..." He rubbed his head thinking fast. "I... don't... like letting other people know. I'm really bad at being a Jai. I always keep losing my luminblade and things," he fibbed. A little white lie, he reasoned, wouldn't hurt anybody.

Janice gave him an odd look, digesting what he had just said. She brushed some bright golden bangs -*the lighting must be better here* – over her ear and nodded adjusting her purse over her shoulder. "That makes sense to me. If my hair doer droid didn't have a voice activated feature, I'd lose it all the time. For the life of me I still can't find my spaceship keys! I lose important things all the time, so I can see where you're coming from," she said tapping her chin looking up at him.

Yurri let out a huge mental sigh of relief. It was a good thing Janice was a blond. He would be in big trouble if she were something more intelligent like a brunet or (*shudder*) a red head. -*It had to be the lighting or his mind playing tricks on him!*- "Yeah... I lose things all the time too... Let's keep on walking to the city Jan. I think we lost Ron by now. He doesn't seem too bright."

"Yeah," affirmed Janice as they started making their way in the direction they thought would get them back to the city or at best to Yurri's hover car. "Ron never was the brightest glow rod out there. I felt sorry for him about that too. One time, at a drive through, the person that was taking our order was a really snotty teenage boy." Janice went on to explain how Ron, becoming infuriated, told the boy he would kick his can if he didn't apologize to him. This teenage boy continued making rude comments of Ron and Janice. Ron leapt out of the hover car and throttled the speaker system leaving it in pieces. He got back in his hover car saying that that should teach a droid to be snotty with him.

Janice chuckled at Yurri covering her mouth. "He did things like that all the time. I'm still surprised that he can even dress himself properly *by* himself." she finished, giggling again into her hand.

Yurri gave a small polite laugh with her, shaking his head wondering to himself, *and this coming from a girl who actually locked herself in her own hover car?* He had to walk her through how to open the door herself. She thought she had locked herself in the hover car without her keys. The ironic part about that was that the keys were still in the ignition.

With that said and done the couple went on to finding a trail. Yurri didn't like to boast, well he rarely did not like to boast, to his friends anyways, but he had a sense of direction as keen as any global positioning system. He led the way in trying to find the park again, so they could determine where the city was. The park they had been in before Janice's old boyfriend showed up was a bit away from the city.

As they made their way through the forest Janice started picking flowers in an unconcerned manner and started making a wreath. This perturbed Yurri a little bit. How can she be so calm while he was at risk of getting some inconsiderably uncomfortable things done to him if her old nut job boyfriend found them? She was humming a playful tune as she was working the flowers into a lei shape.

"Uhh Jan," Yurri said as he ducked under a low branch pulling it out of the way for her.

"Yes? Ow!" replied Janice pricking a finger with a thorn at the same time as she ducked under the tree branch. She stuck that finger in her mouth looking at Yurri in a very cute way with a question on her face.

It took a moment for Yurri to come out of admiring Janice's cute beauty with her sucking on her index finger.

"Umm," he said letting go of that branch with a smile he couldn't help on his face. "Don't you think it counterproductive to give Ron a trail to follow us?"

"What do you mean?" she asked still sucking her finger. "I'm not leaving any trail that Ron could ever follow." Yurri pointed to her wreath in the works then waved a hand over the area she last picked some flowers behind them. "Oh that," she said recognizing what Yurri meant while brushing back some dark blond bangs *-it must be the lighting again–* from her face. "Ron can't find himself out of an indoor park," she laughed dislodging some dark blond bangs from her face again.

She suddenly grabbed Yurri's arm. "Oop, don't step on that plant!" She pointed to a small patch of blue bulbous plants that smelled a little like burnt meat. "Those mark a small colony of fire lintches," she explained while they stepped around the small cluster of those plants. Yurri gave her a blank look as she led him. Taking his silence as an invitation to proceed with her explanation she continued as they walked holding his arm leading him. "Lintches are nasty small insects that need a lot of protein. Those blue plants back there are chalk full of protein so the lintches grow them to feed their colony. If a lintche bites you that appendage will start going numb. Anything they catch bothering their colony they eat alive. Yes, I know, not a very pleasant way to die. Why are you looking at me like that?"

Yurri tried to swallow his amazement, clear his face, and said, "You apparently have a lot of knowledge about this planet. Where did you learn all of this?" Yurri had only moved to this planet two years ago while Janice only had lived here for about nine months. How did she know more about it than him?

"I like to know a little about the planets that I'm currently living on. Don't you?" She smiled at him in an almost condescending way still working on her wreath. She happily kept on talking bringing up their last subject. "I very much doubt Ron would be able to find us in a forest. He has more brawn than brains, as I've told you earlier, and he is otherwise an asinine puppy when it involves other subjects not akin to bounty hunting or beating up a poor individual. His behavior is quite vexing for me. That's one of the many reasons why I broke up with him."

Yurri shook his head again. She now sounded like a professor lecturing a simpleton. And her hair was very dark blond now almost a light black. He stopped where he was looking at her in a perplexed manner.

"What's the matter?" she asked stopping with him looking worried. "Do I have a bug on my face or something?" She brushed her cheeks worriedly.

"Umm," he said still looking at her. How to put this? "My eyes must be playing tricks on me or something," he reasoned out loud while lightly taking a strand of her soft and almost jet-black hair bringing it up to look closer at. Janice flinched visibly seeing her hair dropping her wreath. "But for some reason your hair looks…" Yurri wasn't able to finish for Janice was firmly pressing her infinitely soft and alluring lips to his while seductively pressing her wonderfully shaped body into his pushing him up against a tree.

After a couple more moments of pure bliss for Yurri she drew herself away and started swatting at her hair decoration for some reason, muttering angrily. Yurri didn't notice any of it. His back rubbed the tree as his legs wouldn't hold him erect anymore.

After a couple minutes in a merry daze something finally woke Yurri up. That something was rubbing his neck and shaking his head. The poor fellow, Yurri, brought up his head with a smile that seemed locked into place on his face. Everything was blurry in his sight and it took a couple moments for his eyes to adjust to see the woman who was kneeling at his side looking worriedly at him. "Are you ok Yurri?"

"Yeah I'm fine," he replied with that silly grin still on his face. "Why wouldn't I be?" Who was this again? Oh yeah, it's just Janice.

"Well you kind of collapsed on me," said Janice as she pulled some now blond bangs out of her eyes again. Now blond? Why would they be now blond? Her hair was always blond. Has been since the first day he met her. It's her natural hair color of course wasn't it? It was hard to remember the past few days for some reason.

"What happened?" Yurri asked. *And why do I feel so happy about it?*

Janice smiled mysteriously as she helped Yurri stand up again. "A rock fell out of nowhere and hit you on the head," she said looking like she was picking out her words carefully.

When Yurri was finally on his feet he looked around wobbly. They were in the forest. Why were they in a forest again? Oh yeah, to try and escape from Ron, Janice's old mad boyfriend. Getting that thought out made Yurri dizzy after the concentration it required to retrieve. "Are you ok Yurri?" Janice asked him while helping him to keep his balance.

The poor boy looked around dizzily trying to organize his thoughts properly. They were in a forest. Where did a rock come from? Probably it came from one of those mean looking trees. He looked at the nearest tree with an accusing glare still not having his wits about him.

All of a sudden, an explosion could be heard from not too far away. It shook the ground where they stood, and a few leaves dropped out of some trees making small animals shriek and run for cover. "Uh oh," Janice said stepping back from the direction of the boom. "Ron must be getting frustrated. He is trying to flush us out."

Yurri's head may have been in the clouds before but a jostle from an explosion not too far away shook something straight in his head. "He's trying to flush us out with *explosions?*" Well she did tell him that Ron wasn't the brightest glow rod in the bunch, but this?

Janice looked up at him with worry on her face biting her lip. "Yeah, he one time got so frustrated looking for a group of guys in a labyrinth of a huge building that he just started setting explosives all over the building and setting them off. He scared those fellows so badly they surrendered to him after several explosions. I think they thought Ron was going to topple the whole building on them." Another explosion went off. The two jumped looking in the direction the roar came from. This was closer than the last one. Janice trembled holding her arms and continued her explanation stepping closer to Yurri. "It worked so well for Ron he has been using it ever since. Most of the time, now, his marks just surrender themselves to him if they know he's in the same building with them."

Yurri's thoughts seemed to rush through sludge. Maybe it hadn't been a very good idea to date a girl who out of the blue said yes to a date with him and hasn't broken up with him yet over months of dating. He shook his head trying to clear his thoughts and looked at Janice. "Hey, we need to find a place to hide before your nut-case old bounty hunter boyfriend finds us."

"I can help you out with that, but only for a price," said a deep voice out of nowhere.

Yurri nearly jumped out of his pants from fright. "Who the heck are you and where did you come from?!" Yurri asked the short newcomer while pulling his pants back on. Good thing they caught around his knees.

"Hello my good fellow. My name is Tom Finney. I have a science lab not too far away from where we're at right now."

Yurri gave the short slightly graying mousey brown-haired scientist a bewildered look and asked him sounding doubtful, "So you have a science facility nearby?" This guy even had the stereotypical white lab coat on though it did look dirty and worn too much.

"Yes. Yes I do."

Yurri gave the odd little man a cynical look. "How'd you find us? What do you do, listen in on people's private conversations and erratically jump out to scare them?"

"Yes," came out the strange man's surprising reply. "A man must have his hobbies or you're apt to go mad from loneliness."

"Uhh... yeah sure, we'll go with that," said Yurri giving the weird man that odd look again, cocking his head.

"Yurri we need to find a place to hide from Ron. The last boyfriend he found me with went from a bass singing voice to a low soprano." Janice's sentence was punctuated by another explosion. Yurri gave Janice a very surprised and worried look at her about that. This was getting way too out-of-hand for poor Yurri. It sounded like death would be a better option than being caught by her crazy old boyfriend.

"Come; follow me to my secret lab." The small peculiar man waved a hand bidding them to follow him.

They followed the curious man through the foliage to an odd-looking boulder with some scratches on it. The short scientist traced a finger from one scratch to another going from the top down in a Z pattern. "Come and stand by me please," the man bade Yurri and Janice. After his guests were standing beside him, he knocked three times on the boulder and suddenly they were going down. Janice jumped with fright and firmly pressed her soft body up against Yurri's causing the lei she put on his head to fall off. Janice had put it on Yurri's head while making that short walk with this odd scientist.

The ride down actually wasn't that long to Yurri's displeasure. He was really enjoying himself very much with having Janice holding him so closely. When the elevator door, opposite to where they had entered, opened they went through it. Before they started out Yurri reluctantly let go of Janice. He wished he could hold her like he did last time. Last time? What happened last time she had been this close to him? That rock must have hit him pretty badly, but though, now that he thinks about it, his head didn't even hurt.

As all of them stepped out of the elevator there was a big mat in front of the elevator that had big words printed on it saying, "Wipe your feet!" The weird scientist man named Tom reflexively wiped his own two feet on it then started walking down the hallway. Yurri followed the man's example shortly getting done but Janice lingered a tad too long while their host merrily made his way down these metallic, somber, and undecorated hallways. Yurri patiently waited for Janice as she looked like she wanted to physically take off her shoes and brush them off. "Come on Jan," Yurri said getting impatient as their host rounded a corner ahead going out of sight. "You can clean off your shoes later!" He grabbed her hand pulling her up as she was meticulously getting out every grain of dust in her shoes. "Those are your outside shoes anyways! They're meant to be gettin' dirty!" They both ran to catch up with Tom which they did quickly enough.

The professor quickly led them to his lab going down through some metal hallways which took them quite a while. When they arrived and entered the strange scientist's lab Yurri and Janice quickly noticed that this guy had a holo-art gallery filled with loads of images that neither Yurri nor Janice knew how to react properly to and still be polite guests.

"Ahh, I see you two are admiring my girls," the weird scientist said. "It gets very lonely down here and these holos keep me company." Tom Finney gazed around this room with a hungry look on his face. "Here, let me show you a couple of my gems before we get started." He led them deeper into his strange art gallery. "These are my most prized holos," he said while pointing to some holos that had their projectors specially decorated.

"So these are your most prized holos?" Yurri asked with a tone of marvel in his voice while wondering where in the worlds this guy got all these images.

"Yes! Yes, they are! Just look at those curves," Tom said while motioning his hands over the areas he was describing. "And look how soft and smooth these girls' skins look. Also notice what they're wearing and how it form fits to them accentuating every luscious *curve* and *bump*! The most intoxicating thing that I can imagine about these girls that I can't get from these holos is their smell. I would just love to touch and feel them having their intoxicating scent fill my nostrils."

Yurri was having serious doubts whether or not it was a bright idea to follow this guy. This dude had a serious problem with women's feet!

He looked about again and took in what was around him slowly. Feet of all different shapes and sizes surrounded them. Humanoid feet were way more prevalent than any other type of foot. As the wacky scientist continued their tour Yurri thought he even saw a huge furry Gytan foot! And this loon wanted to be able to smell these feet too?!

"Umm, Professor Tom?" Yurri interrupted the mad scientist's tour of his insane obsession with women's feet.

Mr. Finny gave Yurri a confused look at first coming out of his pleasant reverie. "Oh, I'm sorry! I'm taking up too much time while you have an insane bounty hunter after you two. It's just that after so many years alone with no company I would give anything to have those sexy, alluring, and intoxicating appendages flounced in front of my face. Or just to fondle their toes between my fingers. I could die right then and there a happy man."

This dude is seriously disturbed, thought Yurri. "Uhh yeah sure, it's every guy's dream to have smelly feet shoved in front of their faces."

"Isn't it now?" The wacky man led them through deeper into his laboratory. "Here milady I think you would be more comfortable in my dressing room whilst I take your boyfriend and fill him in on what I want you two to do for me in return of my protection." He pointed to a door that slid open.

Janice warily made her way into the room and once she was fully in there she shrieked with delight. Yurri promptly rushed in through the door to see what all the excitement was about. What he saw was a messy room full of dress up gowns that had an assortment of frills and pretty bows sown into them with a few tuxedos in the corner.

"Ohh mister nice mad scientist man sir, may I please try on some of these on while you are away with Yurri please?" Tom Finney gave her a puzzled look, so Janice tried to make herself more clearly understood. "The dresses that look like they were made for noble women," she said while pulling on a sleeve of a dress, holding it up.

"Huh, so these are the type of garb noble women wear. No wonder they felt so uncomfortable and awkward when I tried them on." The professor straightened his lab jacket as if remembering the uncomfortable fit. "I was going to have them all sent back, but I got too distracted with my work and my hobby to do so. I really should lodge a formal complaint to the post office and tell them that they really need to have those delivery droids looked at for problems." Tom shrugged. "Yes you may try them on if you want to my dear. Though it will only take me about an hour at the very most to explain to your boyfriend what I want him to do for me."

Janice came up to Yurri and tantalizingly brushed her long slender fingers lightly behind his left ear. "Please, take your time, dear." She tickled his chin for a moment before going back to look at the dresses. Yurri just stood there with a dazed happy look on his face.

"Ok my friend it's time for me to explain to you how you can repay me for my help." The scientist started walking away. He had gone a little way away before he realized that Yurri wasn't following so after an uncomfortable confrontation having to wake Yurri up they continued. The young man wiped some drool from his face and started to follow Tom.

It wasn't a very long walk through the metal corridors, but it did take a while, this place was huge! The scientist brought Yurri into his big lab area that smelled heavily of electronics and chemicals with an overlaying sooty smell of animal habitats. This place was enormous (as earlier stated)! The scientist told him to wait by the entrance and not to touch anything whilst he went to grab a couple items Yurri would use to repay the scientist for his help.

It was a mistake for Mr. Finney to leave Yurri here all by himself. For this boy had an almost fatal habit of going through things he was specifically told not to touch. This was one of the reasons why he had to move to this planet in the first place, for he had originally wanted to become a militia man like his father. He was put to the task of guarding experimental weapons and battle droids. Having an ADD moment he got curious about what the controls to certain devices did. Needless to say it did not end very well for him. At a threat to his life from the commanding officer there his parents shipped him off to Drylon 3, getting him a job at an old friend's well-off restaurant and the rest was history.

The room he was in was enormous full of all types of science components. There were also small and large cages full of experimental animals not too far away from the entrance.

The cages the animals were in were labeled with signs on the front of them showing things as "Experiment 244" and the like. One caged experiment in particular caught Yurri's interest. It was one of the larger animals. Yurri always liked looking at the bigger animals in zoos. The creature looked like a giant cat with furry orange scales. Half of its face was a huge maw which had serrated fangs as long as Yurri's forearms.

Being the not so bright fellow that Yurri was he wanted to see how this monstrous creature looked when it was standing up, so he started looking for something to throw at it. It was safely in a cage, so he believed it couldn't hurt him if it noticed him. He picked up a small rock from the edge of another cage and returned back to the other cage at a safe distance away. After missing a couple times, he generally was a bad aim; he started to get frustrated. He had gathered a small pile of rocks by then from that other pen and was trying to lob them at the huge creature unsuccessfully so far.

He continued to approach the cage as he continued to miss his target, shoving his pile of decent sized, for the job, stones forward with a foot. He was nearly touching the cage by the time he finally hit the large beast on its nose. Yurri, the clueless goober, waited in expectation for the beast to wake up. Frowning when the beast didn't stir, he bent down to pick up another stone to toss, but when he stood up he found the creature eye to eye to him staring at him.

Yurri nearly wet himself. It was a monster it was so huge. He hadn't realized he had gotten so close while throwing rocks at it. He could feel its breath on his face. Oddly enough to Yurri its breath somehow smelled like cabbage, weird to say the least.

The poor shlub started to back away very slowly. The beast sneezed which made Yurri back pedal in a panicked wobble, he never was very coordinated either, until he collided into another cage. He fell on his side with a grunt his head swimming.

After a moment or two of lying there his thoughts finally came back to him. He stood up shaking his head and looked around making sure everything was in order. It wasn't.

There was a cage wide open with a lot of foliage and dirt in it. It was one of the larger cages about the size of the dining room in the restaurant where he worked. He ran to slam it shut again. As soon as it was closed a fortifying blue energy shield enveloped this whole cage rapidly. When it was shut, he couldn't help noticing a large sign on the door of it. It said, "Take caution, the contents of this cage are extremely dangerous. Experiment #666." Yurri took a careful look into the cage itself, walking a few paces away from it, and couldn't see anything in all that brush. Maybe it was hiding, he hoped. An animal the size of a Nixdon bear could hide easily in that huge cage with all that shrubbery and trees. He turned to look back at the critter that sneezed on him feeling very wary. If that monster didn't have a warning sign on its cage, or an energy shield also, what type of creature might be in that other cage he bumped? He prayed that it was still in there.

"So you're admiring my pets, are you?" Yurri clawed himself into the air about three paces landing firmly on his bottom afterwards with a gulping yelp. The scientist looked down at him smiling a complimentary smile. "That was a good jump. The highest I've ever seen someone go before was about two and a half paces in the air."

Yurri quickly stood up rubbing his bottom glaring at the absurd man. He *actually* measures how high people jump when he scares them?! This was a loony man to the core. "Uhh yeah I was just looking at this monster you have caged there," he said pointing at the animal that sneezed on him. "I've never seen a cat-like creature with serrated teeth before.

What does it eat?" He hoped that this subject would keep the scientist from noticing any of his other science experiment cages.

"Oh you mean PAT. He eats local flora."

Yurri gave the scientist a dubious look. "It's a vegetarian?" His voice drizzled with doubt. With canines like that this guy wanted him to believe that this monster ate plants? He really was insane.

The fellow took in Yurri's doubtful looks and grinned. "Yes, I know at first glance PAT looks quite fearsome, but he is actually quite placid most of the time. Here, let me show you what I designed him to do." The mad scientist clapped his hands and yelled out for a droid to come and bring PAT some food. A metallic cone shaped droid floated into the room carrying a small tree which it had latched to it by three metal looking cords. The mad scientist ordered the drone to drop the small tree into PAT's cage. It flew over PAT's cage and a ringing sound came from it. The top hatch of the cage opened up to let it drop that small tree in. PAT had been eyeing that small tree looking excited since the droid flew in with it. Yurri gave the scientist that dubious look again when PAT didn't do anything but look at the log intensely. He opened his mouth to comment on this, but he didn't get a chance to. PAT ferociously lunged itself at the small tree and brutally tore into it.

Yurri's mouth dropped open as he witnessed this terribly gruesome scene. Mr. Finny chuckled at Yurri's expression and explained how PAT was designed to clear out forested areas for construction. There were only a few problems he had to weed out, first such as PAT wasn't able to stop attacking trees until there were none left, or it ate so much it died. He chuckled again and looked at PAT affectionately. "Well it looks like you avoided bumping into any of my cages. Since I don't get too many visitors here all these cages have a simple push button opening device on each of them. Better for my back to not have to wrench anything. But we didn't come here so that I could show you my pet projects," Tom smirked at that putting a hand in his right lab coat pocket. He brought out two different colored cologne looking sprays one red and one blue. "These are what I want you to test for me."

This made Yurri pause looking very dubious again at Mr. Finny. "You want me to try on cologne you made yourself?" he asked shaking his head. "Dude, you can get deodorant at the local mart cheap. I use Aximp. You know the one. Made strong enough for huge furry Gytans they say," he said taking the baggy of those items after the mad scientist put them both in it.

Tom shook his head. "This isn't your everyday run-of-the-mill type of cologne my friend." He explained that since he was too shy to approach a human female to ask her out on a date, he devised a way to attract females from another species entirely. He told Yurri that he found the perfect alien species too with the most wonderfully exotic beautiful feet he's ever seen. "Another reason why I've chosen them is because they select their mates through smell not looks. They don't seem to like humans very much. They think we stink." He shrugged and made a comment about different species being different.

I wonder how these aliens look, Yurri thought to himself.

The mad scientist continued. "So I've devised a way to 'attract' a female for myself. Here let me show the intoxicating sight of them." He brought out a small holo-projector disk from his pocket and turned it on. What came from that holo-projector made Yurri's jaw drop. It was a very humanoid looking alien female with light red skin and blue hair. She wore a very well form fitting green gown that accentuated and emphasized every round curve on her. It was almost indecent, considering that parts of it were translucent ranging on transparent especially in the midsection area. The only figure he knew of that could be on par to rival this figure was Janice. The face of this alien woman was also astounding to look at by human standards too.

Yurri just gaped and ogled at the holo figure in amazement. "Wow... Just wow," Yurri said in astonishment.

"Yes aren't they wonderful?" the mad scientist said grinning at him. "These aliens have what normal human women lack." He waved a hand under the holo's feet, which Yurri noticed for the first time of course. Tom Finny zoomed in the holo on the alien's feet. Apparently, she was shoeless, which Yurri was too distracted to notice before. This alien woman had eight toes on each foot! Her feet looked like it would be hard to comfortably get shoes on with those extra toes. Yurri thought it was a good thing she was wearing sandals because he couldn't think of any type of shoe that would fit comfortably on those feet.

Yurri's eyes were magnetically drawn up to the higher regions when the scientist laid out his plan to him. It took a couple tries for poor Yurri to take the mad scientist's plan in all the way. It helped when Tom turned off the holo disk and gave it to him. Just so he could be sure he found the right species. "Something else I think I should mention to you is that if you sweat it would intensify the cologne's effect tenfold. So as long as you remain calm and don't decide to go jogging with the cologne on, I think you'll be okay," the mad scientist put in finally in an off handed way. After the plan was explained enough Tom led Yurri back to where Janice was trying on clothes.

Yurri didn't talk on the walk to where Janice was. He was too busy working on an ulcer in his stomach thinking about how to explain the "help" they were going to give the wacky man Tom. Tom had told him, in an off handed kind of remark again, that he had no idea how the alien females would react to the cologne. For all he knew it would enflame the women into a frenzy that would have them fighting tooth and nail to take him for themselves getting his clothes ripped off in frenzy or they might just wink at him blowing him a kiss with some suggesting looks. Tom had sounded like he was explaining a grocery list he wanted Yurri to get him, a list with very desirable ingredients that the mad scientist wanted as soon as possible, but still in a tone that expressed not much more emotion than that.

As they walked through the mad scientist's lab down more hallways. *—Why does this loon need so much space?—* Yurri thought up something to take his mind off telling Janice what this guy wants him to do. "I noticed that PAT's name was capitalized. Is his name an acronym?"

The man gave him a weird look. "I didn't have PAT's name posted anywhere. How did you know that its name was capitalized?"

"Well ummm..." Yurri had no idea how he knew that. It just sounded capitalized. "It... It just sounded capitalized that's all. The emphasis you put on it gave it away I think."

The small man gave him that odd look again shaking his head. "My friend, I have to tell you that you are the strangest man I have ever met." Yurri stared incredulously at Tom. This coming from a man who worshiped women's feet and randomly jumps out scaring strangers? "Anyways I'll tell you why PAT's name is an acronym. PAT is an acronym for Pathologically Attacks Trees," he said with a smile looking proud. "It took me a whole month to think up that acronym. This way makes it easier for me to remember what all of my experiments do. Otherwise I just number them. The more dangerous they are the higher number they get. I've only gotten to six hundred and sixty-eight so far. Ah here we are." Tom tapped on a button to open the door and they went in.

The first steps that Yurri took into this huge closet his mind was full of worry, but when he finally took in where he was at his jaw fell open. It looked like the place had been torn through, organized, torn through again, and then organized again! Like a hurricane that thought to organize its mess up afterwards went through here! All the dresses and skirts were arranged by color and size. The men suits were all nicely trundled up in a corner. There seemed to be much more suits now than he noticed before. What in the worlds did this solitary scientist use all those suits for anyways?

After this initial shock Yurri noticed something that almost floored him. It was Janice who was wearing what seemed to be like a very white and traditional looking wedding dress. She was twirling around in front of a mirror that he hadn't noticed in here before with a big smile on her face. This closet was gigantic!

After her second twirl she noticed them. She came walking up to them slowly with that big smile still on her face. Yurri could not take his eyes off her for worry about what her thoughts might be at that moment. It also didn't help that the dress had a deep plunging neckline too.

Janice walked directly up to Yurri putting her hand on his chest looking to him for the entire universe like the happiest bride to be and looked up into his eyes with her big pouty blue eyes that could very well swallow his soul. "You know Yurri I've been thinking about our relationship and all the things we've been going through lately." Yurri did not like where this seemed to be going. "And I thought we need to do something more to cement our relationship." *Oh no!* "I got this idea from the dress I'm wearing right now." *EEP!!* "Can you guess what I'm thinking about doing dearie?" she said while stroking his cheek.

Blood was rushing through Yurri's head, he could hardly hear anything else except his thundering heartbeat, and he found it hard to stand upright. Janice frowned at him worriedly looking like she expected an answer. "You, uhh, want to go out shopping with me so we can get me a tuxedo so we can go out to a ball room dance?" he said lamely shrugging, quirking a weak crooked smile.

She smiled looking a little surprised while patting his cheek. "I really thought you weren't going to get it on the first try. We've never been out dancing before so when I saw this dress, I thought we should do something like that: after we get through all this madness of course. Whoa, are you all right Yurri?"

Poor Yurri nearly had collapsed from relief. Janice held him up until he leaned against the nearest wall, panting. "Sure Jan," he said. "It's just a surprise to me that you want to take our relationship to that next level."

"Well I've never dated a Jai before. Even though you've never shown me any of your powers, you've kept that hidden pretty well from me, I expect you to show me some of your tricks in the future," she said cuddling up to him almost uncomfortably.

"So you're a Jai too." Yurri jumped a little and Janice stepped back when she finally noticed the nutty scientist. "Well that doesn't change anything. I can hardly believe that anyways though I do find it a bit peculiar under your circumstances." Tom looked up at Yurri tapping his cheek for a bit then turned to Janice. "You may keep that garment if you want my dear. My closet is getting too crowded anyways." He waved a hand around for emphasis. "Besides which I didn't like the fit of that much myself. Even if they do send you something by mistake it's always a good idea to try it out for quality."

"Oh thank you Mr. Tom!" she said hopping and clapping her hands. "But how will I carry it with me? We need to avoid certain people and I don't think Yurri would like to be carrying my dress for me if we have to run." She gripped her skirts drawing them up for emphasis.

"Oh you don't have to worry about carrying it my dear. I'll loan you one of my portable wardrobes. It's an older model anyways, but it can still come in handy for you. It's the least I can do for you after you so expertly organized my closet for me." Tom started shuffling through some hanged shirts to get at something behind them. He came out from all those clothes with a black flat cylindrical looking disk on a couple straps. "I had a harder time making the newer model, which I have on right now; of course I had to figure out how to get it to register the proper brain waves first for me." The odd little scientist brought it up to Janice and gave it to her looking at her expectantly.

She held it out, dangling from her fingers, at arm's length looking doubtful at it. "What am I supposed to do with this?" she asked.

Tom slapped his forehead. "Oh that's right. You'll have to forgive me. I've been out of touch with the outside universe for so long I don't have any idea how the things I make affect people. For all I know the Kaiser Kahn could have gotten married and is raising evil little Kahns himself right now." Tom shrugged and frowned at both Yurri's and Janice's puzzled and blank looks. He continued on undisturbed anyways. "Do you know the company Syndex?"

"The company that makes all those crazy electronic devices, like the Molt Aid for reptile-like aliens?" Yurri reasoned out.

"Yes that's the one." Tom nodded at him. "They should have my latest device out right now. I think they've been calling it the PC2."

"The PC2?!" Janice jumped giddily clasping the device to her bosom. "You mean you're the guy who makes those?" she asked pointing to Tom smiling in surprise.

"Yes. Yes, I am. I actually own that company too, but I let my company aides do all the business for me. I just don't have the time to run Syndex myself. Too busy with my experiments and my hobby to put in the extra effort to run it," he said looking glum. "This is one of the many reasons I need your help."

Yurri looked down on the little man and his girlfriend with a perplexed look on his face. This loon owned the most productive and successful robotics company on the planet? This does explain why this fellow can afford such a place like this. Well maybe later he could milk the guy for something more after helping him out. Janice was still bouncing happily at his side. What was a PC2 anyways?

"That older model you have is the original prototype for the PC2 so it should have a lot more space within for you to use. Good enough for twenty sets or more of clothes I believe," Tom told Janice.

Janice squealed happily, jumping up and down clapping her hands. "And you're saying that I can put this dress in it too? Oh if only I were at home right now. I'd put all my favorite clothes in here."

Yurri only stood there scratching his chin. That little strap thing had to do something with clothes. He could not see how anyone could wear that thing and feel decent. Maybe it was a backpack of some sort. If it was, he had no idea what or how it held stuff.

The mad scientist chuckled at Janice's outburst smiling appreciatively at her: blushing a little. Maybe he didn't get too many praises for his work. That would make sense since he's holed up in this lab of his most of the time. "My dear since you've shown me just how much my work is appreciated here, I will allow you to take as many garments from my closet as you want. I don't wear them all that much anyways. But my mother always taught me to be prepared for anything when it comes to clothes so here it all is. You need to remember to take my mother literally may she rest in peace." He said that last bit with his head down in a prayerful manner.

    Janice squealed again, bouncing up and down, and gave the mad scientist a kiss on his forehead. He blushed fiercely and pointed to a chamber where she could change. After pointing the way for Janice Mr. Tom Finny motioned to Yurri to follow him. "Let me show you how you will be guided to the place I want you to accomplish the task which I've asked you to do for me."

    The mad scientist led Yurri deeper through his lab and not too far away this time. A solid mechanical door slid open when the scientist waved his hand over a control panel and they entered a room that was hard to describe. This room was huge, just like every other room in this large underground hidden laboratory, and it looked something in between a manufacturing line and an electronics store. This place was chockfull of all sorts of random electrical wirings, disks, chips, metal plates, robotic armatures, robotic chassis, anything and everything to even deal with robotics on tall shelves packed high. This machinery shop even had some large moving robotic arms working on random items put on conveyer belts picking random mechanical items from the shelves and using them putting them together. But one of the odd things about this place was that all the conveyer belts here weren't placed in any logical way that Yurri could see. This shop seemed to have been put together almost or most likely haphazardly.

    The size of those conveyer belts was no thing to sneeze at either. Yurri could guess some of them were well over fifty yards long, maybe even longer than that. And all those huge machine arms, more than Yurri could count off the top of his head, all were hooked to the ceiling and amazingly they moved around up there sliding along the ceiling somehow, were intricately putting some sort of devices together and when one device neared the end of a conveyer belt a robotic arm would transfer said item to the beginning of another conveyer belt or even to the middle of another one too. This scene looked quite random and, in much disorder, but the end result to what these arms were making looked quite incredible too. There was a pile of odd looking and intricate devices piled up near the entrance of this room. Yurri could only guess what each device did.

And all the while in this seemingly unorganized production line a five-foot-long cylindrical almost conical purple floating droid went around zipping to and fro parallel to the ground. This droid seemed to have many compartments which it constantly opened and protruded out a metal tentacle claw thing or various other attachments which it used to make modifications on the materials that were being worked on by the much larger mechanical arms. This droid seemed to oversee the production line. For it had many "eye" stalks protruding from the top of its body on either side coming in and out of it just as fast as its tool tentacles looking every which way making sure production was going along as planned. Seemed that the robot was perfectly in sync with the production line.

"UP5! Come over here for another assignment!" the mad scientist yelled out to his creations. That purple floating droid stopped what it was doing and started heading their way. As the droid came their way Tom tried to fill in the continuously confused Yurri. "This, my young friend, is my customizable manufacturing plant for the devices I invent and sell to the public. Whenever I invent something especially popular with the general public my business aids have advised me that I figure out a way get out as many products as possible when said items first hit the shelves. I made this manufacturing plant as versatile as possible. Once my aides are sure what will sell and just how popular it is, they take schematics I give them and build a manufacturing plant separate from the one I have here. And this," he said pointing to the floating cylindrical droid coming by his side, "is UP5. Or Utility Patronage droid number five. Its older versions should be around here somewhere doing tasks I set them to earlier. But all my UP numbered droids are my masterpieces. UP5 is my latest version of them with all the latest functions and necessities already installed in it. Say hello UP5."

Most of its docile white rimed black eye stalks focused on Yurri, it beeped coming nearer to him, and a three fingered claw hand came out from one of its sockets jiggling it in front of Yurri.

"Uhh…" Yurri backed away not knowing what to do. UP5 extended its clawed tentacle again beeping and whistling in an almost disheartened way. Yurri had his hands in front of him in a defensive manner while looking to the scientist for help. Tom gave him a shaking hand signal then the young man caught on. He cautiously pinched the clawed appendage and shook it. UP5 whistled and beeped a pleased sound. "Sooo…" Yurri cocked his head to the scientist. "It can't talk?" he asked knowing that some droids made, especially maintenance droids, can't be programmed to talk.

"Yes," nodded Tom. "I made all my UP units from modified Cosmomaton droids. I'm sure you're familiar with the brand. Four-legged magnetized rolling droids mainly used on deep space faring ships. Ingenious designs really. Being able to repair a large vessel while under fire. Still too many space pirates out there." He shook his head. "These poor droids have all their memory taken up by repair schematics and utilization methods to allow any other communication other than binary beeps and bops." He shrugged accepting the limitations of this tech. "Unless you have a secondary device to translate for you or have trained yourself to understand them like I have of course," he put in.

Tom turned to UP5. "UP5 here are my instructions," he said bringing out a small chip. UP5 floated nearer to its creator and the scientist slipped the disk into the droid. "You got all that?" Tom asked the droid when it was obviously processing the information from the data chip. The floating droid looked to the scientist and gave an affirming beep nodding its body. "Well done then!" Tom smiled patting UP5 looking to Yurri. "UP5 will be your guide and protector while you go on this excursion for me. It will also document any and all reactions you receive from the marvelous alien species I'm sending you out to experiment on for me."

Tom patted Yurri's shoulder motioning the young lad to follow him again. "Come my young friend and let us procure your girlfriend and I can set you two on your way." The scientist and Yurri made the short walk back to those enormous closets again.

Thankfully Janice had changed back from that wedding gown to her own brown blue dress skirt again also with, of course, her purse slung over her shoulder. The mad scientist then showed them to an underground tram system place. "Here now please let us use my secluded underground tram system to get you all to the experiment site as quickly as possible," said the nutty mad scientist as he bade them all onto his high-speed underground transportation vehicle.

Just how rich *is this madman?!* Yurri wondered to himself as he, Janice, and UP5 got into the comfortably seated tram shooting off right away. Soon they were in the forest again after that following the odd UP5 droid. The droid led them around the forest until they came to a clearing at the bottom of the hill they were on. The droid beeped and bopped at them as the couple followed it all the while Janice nodded saying "mmhmm" here and there pretending like she understood the droid. Just one of her eccentricities that Yurri has come to accept. A bit of the way down into the clearing there was a small village or an encampment of some sort. It looked a little like a festival almost with a more permanent look to it though. It was full of many different types of aliens. Of course there were humans wandering around too, -*humans were like weeds, they just grow everywhere*- but they were few and far in-between here.

The droid, turning and focusing on the couple, started beeping waving its tentacles around sounding like it was giving them instructions. The couple looked at it as it continued on. Yurri had that look of confusion on his face again, like he always had on of late, but Janice was nodding her head making "uh huh" sounds with an occasional "mmm" put in there. Pretending again? When the machine was finally done it retracted its tentacles and its entire set of eye stalks focused on them looking like it expected something.

Janice nodded and thanked the droid and started toward that odd alien encampment. Yurri followed Janice with a puzzled look planted on his face yet again. "You'd better pick a type of cologne to use and put it on right now, Yurri. We'll need to have you set when we find those specific aliens."

What? How did she know what they were doing here? She wasn't there when Tom explained it all to him. He gave her a skewed look that she didn't notice while hurriedly trotting to the bizarre encampment. "Wait Jan, how did you know about that crazy scientist's plan for me? You weren't there when he explained it to me."

"Yeah I know." She looked at him still trotting ahead of him. "UP5 explained the whole plan to me back there." The young man slowed down a bit being confused at this. "Come on you slow poke!" She turned around and waved at him walking backwards. "UP5 said that we need to do this pronto before lunch or it might get messy!" Yurri shook his head and stepped up to catch his pace with Janice.

They continued down the small hill at a steady but hurried walk with Yurri more confused than he could ever remember being. How in the worlds could she understand all those beeps and bops from the UP5 droid? Maybe it was better that he didn't know. He knew that some people who worked with droids extensively or some really smart and educated people, like that mad scientist, knew how to understand droid speak but never once did Janice ever give him any clues that she was ever such a person. And those types of people were few and far in-between to boot. This girl had been causing him whole worlds of problems since earlier this morning. It may be a better idea to avoid finding out any more about her. Ignorance was bliss after all.

Yurri brought out the two cologne bottles pondering which to put on first. The scientist said he didn't know how intensely they would react though Yurri was guilty of feeling a little good anticipation at maybe being mobbed by a horde of beautiful alien women. He chose the red cologne, because red was his favorite color.

After spraying his body thoroughly and rubbing it on carefully he turned to Janice, grinning impetuously. "How do I look or smell or whatever?"

Janice looked at him up and down and pinched her nose. "You smell like a dirty sock now. I don't know how a stench like that could attract any women at all. If you ask me, he should have asked me for some tips. This one time…" She kept on like that as they walked downhill to the odd alien festival or whatever it was.

When they entered the area, they wandered around looking every which way. The place was full of all sorts of odd-looking aliens. Some signs were up indicating that droids were not allowed in some areas of this place. That must be why UP5 stayed behind. There were tents all over the place. All of them varied vastly in shape, size and color. A green and purple bird like alien walked on its hands –*or wing ends?*— by them upside down, weird to say the least. The aliens organized themselves into small groups throughout this menagerie. They avoided the small groups of aliens which looked like they didn't want company with anyone else anyways. There were quite a few activities going on throughout the place. Some of those activities only confused the couple more while others made them blush and quickly scurry away. Yurri couldn't see the point to this conglomeration of all these weird aliens. They were having no luck so far in finding those specific aliens and Yurri's feet were starting to hurt.

"Hey there sailor what's your name?" a very sultry and feminine voice came behind Yurri with a slight tap on his shoulder. When Yurri turned around to see who was addressing him he expected to see anything except what he found behind him. A wide long jawed alien was looking into his eyes with huge saucer sized eyes with a sickly green color to its skin. It even had some scales on its neck! "Hey you're cute. Isn't this one a catch Franzise?" The alien said to a friend next to it. He wasn't sure by the way it looked with its oddly shaped body and bumps coming out at odd places, but he thought these aliens were females.

The strange alien female smiled and flounced herself weirdly while tapping his nose in a sultriest way. Her friend tapped a tusk protruding from her mouth – *a tusk!* – while taking him in up and down. "You know I don't usually go for humanoids Natrice but there is something different about this one." Franzise breathed in heavily leaning towards him. "I think he could be a keeper though." Her face split in two showing round large teeth besides the tusks on the lower jaw. Still they both talked in the most feminine and pretty human girl tones. They even had their local accents down pat too. It was extremely off putting for poor Yurri.

"Hey, I think we should share this catch with everyone!" Natrice grabbed his arm with a big hand that could easily palm his head in it.

"Yeah, we shouldn't be selfish and see how we should divvy him up, but we get first dibs, of course!" Franzise chimed in while grabbing his other arm looking into his eyes. "So what's your name cutie?"

"Uhhmm," Yurri said at an all-time big loss for words. How to put this and still be polite? You're not my type. I already have a girlfriend. Did you get beaten senseless with an ugly stick or did you get in a fight with an ugly stick and scare it away? Not the best choice of words for that last question there. "Uhh I'm not sure I'm right for you girls. I'm here with my girlfriend right now," he said pointing at Janice who looked very startled at this occurrence.

One of those terrible looking alien females, Yurri thought it was the one called Natrice, chuckled with that amazingly dulcet voice and made a pouty face, at least he thought it was a pouty face, a strange combination, and said, "I don't think your girlfriend would mind us showing your gorgeous self to our other girlfriends, will you?" That question aimed at Janice ended with a growl and what looked like a threatening smile showing teeth almost bigger and longer than a human's thumb.

Janice put up her hands saying that they could borrow him for a minute or two if she got him back and could follow. The hideous aliens, not polite to call any type of female hideous but Yurri couldn't think of these people any other way, said that Janice could follow them if she wanted only if she didn't get in their way, whatever that meant. They were oddly perky and friendly throughout this whole ordeal yet at the same time quite adamant that Yurri was their find and they had first dibs on him.

The situation was taken completely out of Yurri's and his girlfriend's hands. Natrice and Franzise formally introduced themselves informing them that they were of the race called Enohps, a very talkative species apparently. The two told them that this place was for special aliens with social orders —*or disorders*— too erratic and incompatible with humans, which were the main species on this planet. Therefore some aliens had a whacky idea to form a camp for all the "special" aliens that didn't get along with humans particularly well out in the wilderness but near enough the city to be a part of it also. While they were telling them all of this, they very uncomfortably kept on taking deep breaths near Yurri, as if breathing in his smell.

As these two wonderfully misshapen females escorted Yurri and Janice to wherever it was they were taking Yurri they talked. And not the ordinary type of conversational stuff at all. Yurri expected that the Enohps had a very good reason to be in the place where aliens with weird social orders and customs congregated. Some of the things that they chatted about doing with him would make anyone's skin crawl sometimes literally in fact. After a wickedly long and agonizing time, for Yurri, they arrived where these two females had been taking them. Here is where it all went to lunacy.

Janice panted and sobbed with relief planting her hand on a tree to steady herself. She had never seen such an angry mob before. She was by herself lost yet again in the forest outside of the city. That mob had been after Yurri so as soon as he bravely split off from her, they went after him and ignored her. Not that the blatant disregard hurt her feelings or anything. No not that. Not at all! How could anyone feel comfortable around such ugly aliens? Though Janice could think of a couple things that would improve anyone's looks, even theirs. Some mascara here, mouthwash would work too for a fresher breath, with maybe a little eyeliner, and some serious and extensive cosmetic surgery wouldn't hurt either.

"Boy, that sure was close," a light feminine voice coming from the top of her head said. Janice was nodding in agreement for a moment before she caught herself and smartly smacked her hair decoration again. "Oww! What did I do princess?"

The decoration on Janice's head was a special type of droid that she had acquired as a very small child from her father. "You know what you did Décore! You are supposed to be in standby mode until I tell you otherwise! That little stunt you pulled earlier forced me to think quickly on my feet. Thankfully it worked," she said while adjusting her purse and folding her arms under her ample chest.

"There was no one else around except Yurri and besides that I think you've been holding too many secrets from the poor cutie."

Janice sighed heavily. Décore had always done this since she first got her little droid. Thinking for herself the droid sometimes annoyingly thought and did things independent of Janice's instructions and with the recent excitement she probably felt justified in disregarding her owner's orders.

Janice had a rare genetic disease. When she had been born her hair had been translucent. Her parents had fretted over it greatly and her father, who was accounted for a good inventor himself, had made Décore for Janice so she wouldn't be accounted for bald for most of her life. Without Décore she looked like she had a shimmering aura or something streaming from her head. But with having Décore on her head for most of her life she had grown up with a couple odd mental disorders. Janice could change her hair color to any color she desired. With that ability at hand every time the color of her hair changed so did her personality, to an extent. In such a way that it changed her, most of the time, to the stereotypical type of personality for that hair color. Though she did have enough self-control to maintain her desired personality consciously if she tried hard enough, but it was easier to have Décore change the hair color allowing Janice to maintain the personality she wanted at that time.

"You're only supposed to change my hair color according to my mood when we are around people I'm comfortable with and especially not when I'm in hiding! You know that!" Janice was hiding from her parents right now. A couple years ago her parents had announced to her that they found her the perfect husband, a fat old codger who owned a successful trading corporation. But he had a personality that was very lacking for Janice's tastes. He was shiningly bald too, yuck!

"What are we going to do now princess?" her hair decoration, Décore, asked.

"Change my hair to brunet. I need to think on this a while and I can't do that while a blond," she commanded Décore with more than a little distaste in her tone. Normally Janice wouldn't be caught dead as a blond, she was quite intelligent by herself, but she was on the run from her parents to avoid a marriage she didn't want part of. So since her parents knew that she vehemently hated being a blond she thought up a plan to disguise herself. Become a blond and get a boyfriend that her parents would believe that she would never go out with. It had been months since Janice had allowed Décore to change her hair color since coming to this planet.

Yurri had been so exceptionally plain and normal Janice believed that her parents would never look twice if they saw her with him dismissing her entirely as being their child.

Though Yurri was boring at times he did have a good heart in him. And she couldn't help admitting to herself that as a blond she did seem to have more fun with him. Maybe that old saying was partly true. Maybe blonds do have more fun.

Décore was a very special droid. Besides what she could already do for Janice she could monitor Janice's emotions, one of the reasons for being a hair decoration on her head, allowing Décore to monitor her feelings and adapt her hair color accordingly.

"Alright princess you are a brunet now."

Janice knew that the changes to her personality with hair color change were purely psychological, mostly supposedly, but why should you try to fight for control when you could just order your droid to fix it? As a brunet she placed her right hand on a nearby tree with her left hand going to her forehead with her purse at her side hanging on her shoulder. She had a habit of doing this when she wanted to think deeply. She reviewed her memories of earlier this day, sorting and organizing them. Ron had jumped them in the fashion that he normally would have. With guns a blazing with no thought of the future only the present. Yurri, on the other hand, had seemed so normal and placid in nature at first that she thought their relationship would never last past her needing him to disguise herself, though recently he had shown some surprising mental capabilities. How had he surmised that Ron was thickheaded enough to fall for that lame trick? He had also shown some surprising heroics as he did when he shoved her into some brush, effectively hiding her and leading the mob of ugly aliens away bravely by himself.

Janice shook her head. Here she was trying to think of something to get out of this mess and she could only think about boys. Maybe she should think of where her priorities were right now. It was no fault of Yurri getting them all in this situation. It was her duty as princess of planet Tyy to make sure he didn't get hurt by her using him.

"Princess?" Décore asked. "Where did that dutiful UP5 droid go? He has an interesting sense of humor. Want me to contact him?"

Janice whipped her hand from the tree trunk to her mouth. That was right. The UP5 droid should still be in their vicinity. That droid could be useful. She didn't know the area as well as that droid probably did. "Yes Décore please contact that droid. We'll need his help. It can help us find Yurri." She hoped that he got away from that mob safely.

This planet was notorious for having dead zones for small communicators. So basically no bars here. There were a whole bunch of weird minerals that reflect off radio signals jumbling them up basically jamming communication with smaller devices and other minerals that caused various other problems too. This is very prevalent the more outside the city you go. Luckily for her Décore should have just enough strength to contact a close UP5. No colony would have ever thought to be made here on this moon/planet because of all the problematic minerals it had underneath its core before, but since Drylon, the gas giant itself, had a gold mine of resources on it colonists came to bear the inconveniences this only habitable moon had anyways.

"Will do Princess." Décore made popping and clicking sounds as she shifted her form into transmitter state. Décore had a couple useful transformations, a transmitter form that made her look like a little satellite dish that was placed securely on Janice's head, a miniature spider-like droid form she used if she ever got detached from Janice, and, of course, the ornamental hair decoration form used to help with Janice's hair coloring.

While in any other form Décore could only do one thing at a time. So Janice's hair turned to its natural translucent no color. Without any help from Décore Janice had to think pretty hard to act the way she wanted. But without her droid's help the personality of Janice became child-like, distracted, ignorant, unwary, and basically unable to process anything except on the simplest terms. Janice knew this could happen, but she had planned for this in advance. She had a couple toys in her purse that she kept with her just in case she needed to keep her child-like self occupied while Décore made her way back to Janice's head again. But Janice, in this state, didn't search for any of her toys in her purse. Instead she brought out of it a small purple short furred fuzzy animal. While in that mad scientist's lab with Yurri gone with that guy — *Yurri did take his sweet time like Janice asked*— Janice had explored some of the hallways after she had gone through all those clothes. She had found this little cutie by a wall with a huge gash in it. Its front paw had somehow gotten stuck in that gash. That hallway looked to be in terrible disrepair, almost like it had been attacked by a monster drill. There were gashes like the one the poor little critter was stuck in all the way down the hall. After helping it get unstuck Janice wrapped its poor injured forepaw with a clean slip of sewing cloth and some tape she had in her purse.

It was very friendly afterwards. It was awfully ferret like with long legs that folded up to its side nicely. The little friend had scurried up and around Janice tickling her quite pleasantly kissing her face at times too. Janice played with it on the grassy ground while Décore made her transmission. It usually takes a little while for Décore to have a conversation, even a quick one, with another droid. She was a chatter box when allowed to talk to other droids.

As Janice played with her furry new friend, she discovered that it wore a stretchy collar. It had 666 written on its tag. Janice was kneeling down holding the creature in front of her when she found this and smiled childishly. "I will name you Sixy because you like sixes!" The little friend leaned forward and gave Janice another sweet little kiss. This was so much fun!

Janice's hair flowed from translucent back to brunet. She still played with Sixy not noticing the change yet or she was just having too much fun. "Umm princess?" Décore said lightly tapping Janice's head with a hair prong. It took a little while longer for Décore to get Janice's attention. When the droid finally caught her attention she sighed and safely tucked Sixy back into her purse. "The UP5 droid is coming to us mistress. He should have a better idea how to find Yurri and get us out of this mess. He'll be here in just a moment. I gave him access to my energy output when I transmitted to him."

"That's good to hear Décore. All we have to do after he meets us here is figure out what to do next." Janice also told Décore to change her hair back to blond once the UP5 droid got close enough. She was still in hiding from her parents after all.

The UP5 droid showed up coming in closer and started to talk in those beeps and bops again. Janice understood it though. One of the advantages to having a droid on your head all the time was that Décore could translate what any droid was saying directly into Janice's ears sending soft vibrations through her skull. [It's good to see that Décore and you are not damaged, I saw you running from that mad mob. I need to catalogue that occurrence. Do you know what those aliens were called?]

"They were called Enohps," Janice said trying to be polite. "Hey UP5, do you have any idea where we can start to look for Yurri?"

[The test subject?] UP5 asked in a manly metallic voice. Décore always put her translations in that metallic tone of voice for other droids. She also added a masculine or feminine tone to the droids she thought were those genders. [I have no idea. But we might have a lead if we follow the path of destruction left by those Enohps.] The odd crew left in search of any signs that would help them to locate Yurri.

Yurri panted with exhaustion leaning against a tree as his new companion whipped up a holo-map from his wrist device. The Jai, Yurri didn't know the fellow's name yet, examined his map for a moment then motioned to Yurri to start following him. He hasn't talked to Yurri yet. The man was a little shorter than Yurri, but he had a broad muscular build. Poor Yurri felt he had no choice but to follow the Jai, so he did. After seeing what this guy did a person would tend to submit to whatever they wanted.

Yurri scratched at his armpit as he followed the Jai and pulled out a small briar. He must have gotten that stuck there when he was hanging from that tall tree a way back. One of the reasons that Yurri knew this fellow was a Jai was that he could do that really high Jai jump. The Jai had come out of nowhere, slung Yurri on his shoulder, and jumped very agilely through the trees, escaping that mad mob. He also had one of those laser swords at his side. Yurri wasn't very familiar with those types of devices though. He only thought it was a laser sword thingy because this guy was obviously a Jai. What did Janice call those things again?

"So, ahem, does the guy who saved my life have a name?" Yurri asked tentatively following the man.

"He does," the Jai replied keeping his eyes forward. "You are one lucky man that I was in the vicinity. My name is Rialin Epoch. What, my friend, were you doing out in the middle of the forest being chased by a hoard of Enohps?" he asked glancing at Yurri with a skewed eyebrow.

"Heh," Yurri chuckled in a manner embarrassed. "I'm still trying to figure that out myself." Yurri shrugged as he waded through thick foliage. Maybe that cologne he used was defective. Instead of attracting beautiful alien women it attracted those hideous females. At least he thought most were females. He hoped *all* were females. "My name's Yurri Banx by the way."

The Jai turned around and looked at Yurri. "Hmm I can sense you have a very complicated future ahead of you my friend. Come with me and I'll put you in a safe place for now. For some reason I sense that my mission is somehow connected with you though I have no idea how." The Jai waved a hand at him impatiently and kept going toward his unforeseen goal.

"Humm may I ask what your mission is and how it has to deal with me?" Yurri asked feeling the weight of the seriousness the Jai was putting in his words.

"I really don't know how you would be tangled in this myself," Rialin shrugged eyes still forward on the path ahead. "I just sense that you are somehow connected with this mess. You could be entangled in this by knowing a certain someone or you could just be the right person to have at my side at the right time. Visions and feelings coming from the Archai don't give you specific answers most of the time. The mission I'm on right now has to do with a certain princess that had disappeared some time ago. At first her parents, the king and queen of planet Tyy, didn't think her disappearance was too alarming. Apparently, she has a habit of doing this. Though right now they found out a very bad mobster leader of their home planet found out the princess was missing. This guy has a very bad rap from what I've heard about him, so the king and queen petitioned some help from Master Highquasar. Master Highquasar sent me on this mission because I have adept tracking skills."

They shuffled through the forest coming into a clearing. This clearing was huge. Yurri could see the city at the other end of this huge clearing. The city must have been a couple dozen miles away from the forest. They must have come all the way around the city because Yurri didn't recognize the places he saw.

"There," the Jai pointed to a mansion that Yurri hadn't noticed before. It looked like it had quite a few farming fields all around it. "That mansion belongs to the friend of the king and queen I mentioned to you earlier. I'll keep you there for now until I figure out what to do with you," the Jai said sounding impatient with something.

The two walked the long way into the field until they came into the farm lands around the mansion. There were men and women in bright orange work clothes working the fields with the occasional worker droid there also. They were working over a very wide variety of produce. Fruits coming from trees, underground vegetables which were being pulled out or watered or fertilized, they even had some sort of fungus that had large shades overhead. From what it looked like to Yurri the place was an amazingly productive garden.

"Heh," the Jai chuckled, "since I'm being so free with information with a fellow I hardly know but have a good feeling about I'll tell you a little more about Dism Quantum, the owner of these fields and that mansion there," Rialin said waving a hand over the vast expanse that was Dism's domain. "Dism is my contact here on this planet. This is one of his many farming locales over the galaxy. This place provides about thirty-five percent of the food for Drylon 3 with other various farm plantations of Dism's here of course. The man, Dism, is a very wealthy producer of food for many places. Unlike most wealthy people you might know about Dism is very generous with his wealth."

The Jai kept filling Yurri in on more about this guy for some reason. Rialin seemed to be a very affable fellow, once he had a good feeling about you. The pair made their way through the fields. There were many people working out in these fields. A few of them waved a greeting to the pair as they walked through the harvesting countryside.

The things that have been happening to Yurri lately had his mind spinning. Yurri used the peaceful walk through these huge gardens to contemplate. The two continued making their way to the huge mansion that was overlooking these fields. In the past Yurri had made split decisions that had altered the course of his life. Good and bad, such as him making the very bad decision to mess around with that experimental weaponry, asking Janice out on that first date had been spur of the moment too. He never did anything like that before. He had just had this weird inkling to take up his friend on the dare. He had picked that park where they had that breakfast picnic spur of the moment too first off months ago. He had chosen their eating spot at random also. Janice had come to a liking of it. Yurri was thinking of how he had gotten into this situation reviewing all the events up to this point. He couldn't come up with anything.

"Ok my friend we've arrived." The Jai patted him on the shoulder bringing Yurri out of his reverie.

Yurri looked up and indeed they were about thirty yards away from the front door. "Umm, hey Mister Master Archai Yirujie sir," Yurri said not knowing the formal way of addressing a Jai. "My girlfriend, Janice, is still out there. If you happen by her could you please tell her where I am, maybe bring her here too?" The Jai stood anxiously looking at Yurri while he gave some details and descriptions of Janice.

The Jai sighed and impatiently said he would bring her here if he found her. "I need to get back to my wife... I just heard that she is going through labor with our third child. It's been a whole month since I've seen her last and I want to get this mission over and done with."

Yurri could understand that so he nodded. Rialin eagerly made his way to the mansion door and knocked, placing his hands on his hips and tapping his foot impatiently.

Yurri took in the whole mansion looking up and down with his jaw open. He had been too self-absorbed to notice it before. It wasn't gaudy or overdone. The design somehow portrayed deep humility. Yurri couldn't explain how it was humble, but all its trappings and decorations said this place was house to a farmer. It basically looked like a glorified humbling farmer's house.

The door to the mansion opened and the Jai, Rialin, went in. Yurri kept pace with the Jai and followed him in. There was only a pretty serving woman in a dark serving gown to meet them. She had been the one to open the door. "Would you sirs like to see Master Dism?" the dark-haired maid asked.

The Jai talked to the girl like he knew her, asking her to go get the master of the house, Dism Quantum. The girl swished away in urgency for some reason. Yurri and Rialin waited in silence in the ornamental entrance for her return. The silence felt awkward to Yurri, but he couldn't think of anything to say to start up a conversation with the Jai. In all reality the Jai intimidated him. Rialin gave off an aura of power and fierceness even though he acted friendly.

Thankfully a man promptly met them at the door after that wait. He was an older man with a twinkle in his eye and little gray in his deep red hair. He had on work clothes that you would normally find on a rancher/farmer. Maybe he was one of the workers here.

"Mister Quantum, it's good to see you again," Rialin said with a hand out for a shake.

"Have you made any headway on your search?" the older man asked as he took Rialin's hand and shook it.

"I've hit a bump in my investigation sir. Though I do think I may have a lead on how to proceed." The Jai introduced Yurri to Dism Quantum, the rich farmer, and told about how he had saved Yurri from a mob of Enohps. "Mr. Quantum could you please see it that this fellow is looked over? I must run a quick errand real fast before I get back. I'll be back in a jiffy." The Jai waved, backed up, and hurried himself out the door leaving poor Yurri in another uncomfortable position.

Thankfully Mister Quantum took it in stride. He took Yurri over to where he thought would be most comfortable for Yurri to wait. As Mr. Quantum led Yurri through the huge hallways of his mansion he talked about his godchild, the princess the Jai was looking for. She had always been this willful and spirited like her mother. Quantum had grown up with the princess's father. They were old chums. The father of princess Janiece, apparently that was the princess's name, had been in business with Quantum before he met the then princess of planet Tyy. Her father, Vick, had been with Dism surveying some land to start a big farming community on Tyy. The then princess of the planet, Celina, had been assigned to watch the progress of these new entrepreneurs as they surveyed the land. Apparently, planet Tyy was going through a food shortage and needed some new methods of producing food. Vick had been Mr. Dism's chief mechanic in his farming supplies and his best friend too even though Dism was a decade older than Vick. Vick got enamored by Celina, they fell in love, and the rest was history.

"I would give any man that could get my godchild settled down most, if not all, of my estates. All of my children are grown ups and doing well on their own businesses enough that I don't mind giving my wealth to a worthy lad," Mr. Quantum responded to Yurri's question about whether he thought his godchild was a handful. "My godchild has been a handful for her parents ever since she was born. This planet is the furthest I've been able to track her. Luckily, I have some plantations here to act as my operation bases. She has been running me ragged ever since I started this search of her for her parents. She is a very special girl with some very unique attributes."

Dism paused in his talk with Yurri as they came upon an older maid fussing around with a wall hanging. Dism promptly helped the older maid put the fixture on the wall properly calling her by name and asking how her family was doing. After politely helping his older maid Dism continued showing Yurri the way and filling him in on his godchild. "Janiece was born with an exceptionally rare disorder." Mr. Quantum then related the story of how Janiece's hair was translucent and how she wore a weird hair decoration that adjusted her hair color, compliments of her ingenious father of course. They figured this rare genetic disorder happened to the princess because her late great grandmother on her mother's side had some genetic alterations done to her when she was young and unwed. Apparently, she had been trying to make her lower gas expulsions smell like perfume whenever she had one. Didn't work though. It didn't stink anymore but it did make people around her voices higher for a little while. The princess's great grandmother had her DNA cleaned up before she got married. Or so they thought. Who knows how messing with someone's DNA will turn out over generations?

Yurri just shook his head as Mr. Dism continued on talking, now telling Yurri about his own children and how well they were all doing on their own businesses. To Yurri this princess sounded like a freak. He didn't have a particularly high opinion of royalties in the first place. He believed that they all were snobs that thought of no one else except themselves. This prejudice was ingrained into Yurri by his father. His dad, while in the service of the military, had the misfortune of being placed as a bodyguard for an exceptionally rude prince. Yurri could never get the full story from his father. Something went wrong and the prince got killed. Not when his father was watching over the prince, a few months later. "Good riddance," his dad used to say.

So there was a freak out there that was a princess running around willy nilly from some sort of really bad and evil mobster guy from her home planet. In Yurri's mind's eye he pictured this princess with big ears, a deformed body, eyes that weren't aligned properly with each other, and a huge nose that dripped gunk. She probably was a red head most of the time too. People that came from royal lineage always were inbred freaks. That hair disorder proved it. Well at least how Yurri looked at that subject anyways. Not someone like Janice. He really hoped that Jai would find her safely.

Finally, Yurri and his host arrived in the location where Dism meant Yurri to wait. It looked like a show room with many different and eye-catching objects. The place was decked out with all sorts of different and resplendent things. There were ancient suits of armor, ancient metal swords, and all kinds of different types of objects akin to warfare. There were also displays and models of ancient tools of farming too with live holo-images of people working in the most inhospitable of terrain. Dism seemed to be a man of multiple tastes in art. Yurri had on his marveling and gawking face by this time.

"I will leave you here to enjoy yourself until the master Jai returns from his errand." Dism smiled at Yurri's amazed expression. "Mind you, please don't touch anything for your own protection. I've got all this out for display to entertain a group from the local school, so I've got it under guard. If you need anything just jingle that and today's maid, Annetta, will be here to see to your needs," he said while waving a hand to an intercom looking panel by the door. With that Mister Quantum left Yurri in a room full of valuable, fragile, and rare objects, to his mistake.

The poor fellow, Yurri, did a good job of keeping his hands off things at first, but after about five or ten minutes of keeping his hands to himself he developed a disturbing twitch in his right cheek. He wished he had some cuffs to his hands behind his back it was so agonizing to touch something. His family and people that know this little *disability* of Yurri's just shake their heads and waved a hand around to tell him to not touch anything. This little click of Yurri's only seemed to beset him when vocally told to not touch anything.

Since Yurri couldn't keep himself from touching anything he wisely decided to look at the less fragile items first. His first items of close inspection were weapons, of course. The poor lad tried his very best to put the objects back just as he found them. Only a few of the mechanical weapons went off when he touched them. And only one suit of armor for a three-armed alien got shattered because of this. Yurri somehow shoved all the pieces of the suit of armor underneath a couch in that room to hide it. If only Janice were here, he might be able to keep his hands more to himself. He thought she might have a ball here. She was really into things like these.

While he perused many of the objects in this fantastic exhibit of random items, he came across something odd deeper within the weapons displays. It was an odd sort of cylindrical device. It didn't have a sign by it telling what it was like most of the other items. As he played around with it in his hands, he felt like should know what this thing was, but the object's name eluded him. He investigated one of the ends of it trying to decide what it was when a finger slipped over a button. He heard a snap hiss and saw a brilliant orange glow come from the device. Yurri jerked his head from the orange laser beam smelling burnt hair, his burnt hair. This thing was a luminblade! How in the worlds did that crazy old man get a hold of one these weapons?

Yurri, being ADHD again, played with the device he nearly killed himself with for a little while. After that while he turned it off and clipped the luminblade to his belt and struck a few poses in front of a more reflective glass display. His interest was caught by something shiny, of course, after a few poses. He walked over to where he found the shiny objects and was amazed by what he found there.

It was an entire set up of many different types and sets of jewelry. There were so many different types of gems and diamonds and other very expensive looking jewelry here he thought you could buy yourself a small planet with all of this.

As he was picking through the very valuable and precious items, that he knew he shouldn't be touching, one item in particular caught his interest. It was an intriguingly shaped and beautifully aesthetically pleasing looking ring. Its color changed depending on how the light hit it from sky blue to volcanic red to golden yellow, the ring seemed to be made entirely out of some sort of gem substance, and it curled around itself in an impossible manner. Being the grabby person that Yurri was he picked up this very valuable and unique looking ring to inspect it better. He wandered away from the jewelry display, while rolling the ring through his fingers, measuring its weight. It didn't fit any of his fingers. He thought it was made for a woman. He wholly meant to return the ring to its proper place after he was done looking at it.

The thing that Yurri should have noticed before was the big sign at the entrance to this room. The sign that said "Beware, this room is under the protection of robotic attack mice." This was why the owner warned Yurri not to touch anything for his own safety.

So here was Yurri… somehow blissfully unaware of this fact as he wandered into an area which had very fragile looking vases and other objects made of glass-like materials when suddenly something slammed into his face and latched on scratching that face. Yurri screamed, flailing his arms, squeezing his fists shut, and backpedaling into a table that held the contents of the before mentioned materials.

There was huge crash of glass breaking as the table toppled over. Yurri scrambled around all over the place running in panic as the attack mouse droid bit fiercely on his nose and attacked his face. The crashes and things he ran into didn't distress poor Yurri at this moment. He was in a panicked fury by this time by his assailant.

He had scrabbled himself over to the door by this time, thinking that he could get some help. The little security droid squeezed its jaws onto Yurri's nose making it even more painful to have on there. He collapsed to one knee getting a hold of the vicious little security droid and ripped it off flinging it across the room. He knelt there on one knee with his hands out in front of him with his palms up panting.

"Yurri what are you doing?" someone asked. Yurri looked up and saw Janice looking down at him from the entrance a few feet away. "Oh Yurri," she said putting her hand on her mouth sounding breathless. She came closer looking down at his hands. Why…? "I don't know…" she said looking flustered. "I'll have to think about it first... But I will keep this and think about it for a while." She bent down to take Yurri's hand and helped him stand.

What was that all about? Yurri wondered.

His head still felt a little fuzzy from the recent excitement. He rubbed his nose and found his hand coming off it a little wet. He looked at his hand and found it covered in blood. "Oh! You're bleeding!" Janice put her hand to her mouth again. "Here," she said while searching through her purse coming up to him. "I have some bandages and some healing solvent." She was already dabbing his nose and face with what probably was his old handkerchief wet with healing antibacterial solvent and then quickly applied a sticky bandage on his nose. "How did you get those cuts on your nose Yurri?"

Yurri didn't get the chance to reply for someone at the door screamed piercingly. There was that pretty young maid with both her hands to her mouth looking around. Our poor fellow then took in his surroundings. There were many things overturned and lopsided. Quite a few of the items in this room were shattered into a thousand pieces. Yurri had been so panicked and in pain with that security-bot on his face he didn't notice all the things he ran into knocking them down and or smashing them.

The young maid now was dialing something on a communication device she had in her hands. *Uh oh she's calling for security,* Yurri thought. They needed to get out of here and now.

Janice was sitting in the back of a sturdy hover car while Yurri drove through into the city. This man, whom she had been using to hide herself with, had again shown some surprising tact of mind and ingenuity. She could dare say that she was starting to become actually attracted to him. The way he took charge the moment that maid came in and alerted the guards and the way he so expertly and level mindedly ran through all those hallways leading them out. She was still unclear on why exactly the maid had been so distraught, but Janice searched her memories for a second and seemed to remember the room she found Yurri in being in a complete mess. Maybe Yurri had found a robber in that place and fought him off. That would explain why that room had been in such a mess and the cuts on Yurri's nose and face. Janice thought to keep any further questions to herself to see how all of this played out. After all it probably was only a misunderstanding.

Janice pushed against the bulk that was the UP5 droid and wiped some blond bangs out of her face again. The droid was in stand-by mode now. The hover craft didn't have much space in it. The droid had decided to stay with them even though the testing of that cologne was botched. It told Janice that it would stay with them to collect all the information that it could from Yurri. Janice was grateful that the droid decided to stay with them. For when they ran out the front door of that mansion the UP5 droid had somehow procured one of those heavy-duty hover cars the farm workers used. The droid didn't tell Janice how it got the small service hover car or how it knew to have it ready for them in the first place. UP5 sounded embarrassed to tell the whole story so she let it be.

"Janice," Yurri said up front driving on the single front seat of this rancher's hover car. "How did you find me?"

Now that was an interesting question. Janice and UP5 were following the trail of knocked down trees and trampled foliage thinking and hoping to find Yurri alive and well at the end of the trail. What they found instead was a man that was apparently a Jai, him having a luminblade at his side that Janice recognized. Her Daddy had dealt with some before. He looked really beaten up as though like he had just escaped from a fight. His clothes were all disheveled and he looked winded. He told them that there were some men out there kidnapping everyone that they saw putting them to question. He pointed Janice the way to get to some guy's mansion. They got there and she went in, UP5 stayed outside, and a nice maid showed her where Yurri was when she asked. Apparently, they had been expecting her. The maid had to grab something to clean with, so she said she'd be right back and let Janice in through the door. The rest was history. Janice related this story to Yurri to fill him in as he drove minus any parts about Décore.

As Yurri continued to drive them into the city a bright light flashed and Yurri lost control of the hover car. They crashed into a tree. The next thing Janice could remember happening was being picked up out of the hover car then it all faded as she lost consciousness.

Janice fully woke up in the arms of a big smelly man. It took her a moment to realize what was happening but when she finally had her wits compiled, she acted. She promptly bit into the arm that was carrying her and wished she hadn't. It had a very nasty, salty, and unclean taste to it and it had left an oily feel in her mouth, very unclean oil. She didn't think the taste would go away for hours. But the bite did its intended purpose. The filthy smelly man dropped Janice cursing through his teeth. He probably thought she would stay under for quite a while. She landed on her feet and started running adjusting her purse around her neck so it wouldn't fall off as she ran, thankfully she hadn't dropped it. Her younger brother had once teasingly said not anyone could ever break her death grip on her purse.

She looked around to find Yurri and found him swinging a luminblade at some men. Those men suddenly floated into the air and were flung away. He saw her and ran over to her grabbing her by the arm starting them on a run away from those men. There was a lot of noise coming from around the corner of the nearest building.

Janice took in where she was for the first time as they ran. They were in the city now, in the more residential area where people had yards in front of their blue and gray houses, those houses were built side by side with only a couple yards of space in between. There apparently wasn't anyone around.

This place looked like it was newly built, probably a new addition to the overall part of the city. As she looked over the place, she didn't see anyone. They left the sound of people fighting with blasters behind them. They continued to run further into the city. After a while, and quite a few short blocks later, the couple stopped next to a corner of houses packed together.

The road and streets they were now on were paved. Janice leaned herself against a tree trying to catch her breath. "Where..." Janice gasped still out of breath. She inhaled trying to compose herself. "Where is the UP5 droid?" she asked Yurri. She had taken a liking to that dutiful droid.

"I sent it off to find another hover car for us. I think it understood me. I had to chase after those guys when they took you. I don't think UP5 would have appreciated being in that fire fight with us. I gave it my com's number so it can locate us after it finds something to use," Yurri told Janice as he too caught his breath. "I have to tell you I'm kinda glad that that cuss stayed with us. I don't know what type of information he can find for that crazy scientist from us now that we botched his experiment. I think that's why it's still with us anyways. I just wonder what we should do..." Yurri trailed off looking at Janice with a perplexed look on his face.

"What?" she asked with a touch of worry in her voice. "Is there something on my face or did I get a stain on my clothes?" she said while fussing with her blouse, skirt, and hair.

"No," he replied still looking at her up and down. "There's this weird sound coming from you." He stepped closer looking her up and down again. "I think it's coming from your purse," he said pointing to it. Janice opened her purse and found that Sixy was trembling and moaning a little. As soon as it was out of the purse the little creature promptly jumped out of Janice's hands and ran over to one of the grassy yards.

"Oh, Sixy just needed to use the restroom," Janice said as she blushed looking away from her new pet. "We'll need to figure out a way for Sixy to signal me about that," she said to Yurri looking into, yet another, befuddled look on his face.

"Wait," Yurri said holding his hands up. "What the frell *–strong language there buddy-* is that little thing and where did you get it?" Yurri asked that with his arms folded tapping his right foot on the ground.

Janice blushed. She didn't steal Sixy or anything like that. She had merely picked up a creature in need and kept it with her thinking to make it her pet. She would buy it from that mad scientist if she needed to though she didn't know if he owned it in the first place. What was a good way to explain that to Yurri? "I found it in that mad scientist's lab area." She thought it would be best if she was honest with her boyfriend about this. She kept enough secrets from him as it was. "Poor Sixy had its paw stuck in a huge gash in a wall. I don't think Mr. Tom takes very good care of his underground house or his pets. I found poor Sixy there with its paw jammed into a wide gash in the wall. I don't believe Finny takes very good care of his place or pets…" Janice stopped talking when Sixy came back up to her. She picked up Sixy and realized that she was nervous of how Yurri would think of her now. Usually when Janice gets nervous, she rambles a little repeating herself. She looked to Yurri hoping he didn't hold this against her or had noticed that little slip.

"Humm…" Yurri said as he took a closer look at the animal in Janice's hands. "It is cute, but why did you name it Sixy? We don't need to add any more problems piled on the heap load of the ones we already have," Yurri said in kind of a deeply resigned sounding tone.

Janice smiled, patting his cheek, taking that comment as meaning he accepted Sixy. "I named Sixy Sixy because it apparently likes sixes." After a blank look from Yurri she expounded on what she meant. "He has a collar," Janice said showing Yurri the name tag.

Yurri leaned to look at Sixy's collar grabbing it to inspect it. His eyes grew big as he mouthed "*six six six*" quietly. He went very visibly pale taking a few steps away smacking his forehead. This bugged Janice a little at the weird response from her boyfriend. He was muttering to himself a little way away. He said quietly, barely audible for Janice, "It can't be the same thing. It's just too small!" He came over again and inspected the stretchy collar. "Hey Jan," he said after he was done with his inspection. "We… Need to get going. Come on." He grabbed her free hand and started leading her through the alleyways between the houses.

They continued through the back of the houses doing their best to avoid attention. Janice still had her furry new friend in her arms petting his head. Out of nowhere a dozen men jumped around a corner and grabbed at Janice. That man only grabbed Sixy out of Janice's arms. Janice squawked reaching for Sixy but Yurri was on the ball. He whipped out his luminblade and pulled Janice in the other direction. He ran them around a corner and kept on that course. No one seemed to follow them but Yurri kept them going anyways.

Yurri had to stop when Janice pulled herself free after running past a couple small blocks. She ran back the way they came. "I can't leave Sixy behind! They might hurt him!" she cried when Yurri stopped her wrapping his strong arms around her.

After some unsuccessful attempts to escape Yurri Janice stopped to breath. "Wait," Yurri said with Janice firmly in his arms. "Where is that screaming coming from?"

Janice heard it too. It was coming from where they had been running from. "So," she said to Yurri looking up at his face. "You want to figure out what that is or still cuddle?" she said winking at him pursing her lips seductively. Yurri blushed and loosed his grip enough for Janice to get away. She knew he would do that. Yurri was too sensitive for his own good.

This time Yurri didn't catch her until they both were before the corner of where the screaming was coming from. They both stopped as they saw a hand swing to the ground just around the corner. A man with a horrified expression and bloody scrapes on his face came crawling around the corner. The screams continued behind him. He made it halfway around the corner when he was stopped, only half of him was exposed to the couple. "NOOOO!!!" the man screamed frantically trying to scrabble away from whatever it was that got him. "I WANT TO LIIIIVE!!!" he screamed again as he was dragged backward out of view with pain and panic on his face. "SWEET MOTHER OF MERCY NOOOOO!!! I WANT TO…" That last cry was cut off suddenly with a sharp sound that sounded between a crack and a splash.

Janice had her hands up to her mouth looking very white by this time. She looked to Yurri who had a grim set on his face. They stood there and waited, ready to bolt the instant whatever was causing the massacre to come around the corner. Yurri had his luminblade out ready to defend Janice and him. The screams and moans slowly died out, literally. Janice and Yurri stood there looking too stunned to move for a couple minutes until something came prancing around that corner. It was Sixy!

"Sixy!" Janice yelled running over to her pet. Sixy ran up to Janice jumping on her. Janice sobbed so relieved that her new pet was okay the blond collapsed to her knees hugging Sixy to her bosom.

AN ORBITING DILEMMA

Janice sobbed in relief as she cuddled the cute little bugger. "Hey, wait," Yurri said as he came up to Janice. "What happened to all those guys that were chasing us?" He looked down at Janice as she stood herself up with her new bewildering pet in her arms and her impressive purse over her shoulder. No one came around the corner and it was eerily quiet around there too. "Wait here Jan. I'll go see what happened. Just be sure to start running if anything happens to me." He ignited his luminblade again; it looked like he didn't trust himself to keep it on for long periods of time, and tentatively walked around the corner.

As soon as Yurri was decently around the corner out of sight Janice heard him heaving and making gagging sounds. "Yurri are you okay?" she asked, starting to go to the corner to look around it.

"No Janice!" Yurri cried stopping her in her tracks making her back up a bit. "You stay there," some more heaving and puking stopped him from saying anything else for a moment. "It's a mess back here... I don't think you want to see all of this," he continued as soon as he could.

A couple minutes passed for Janice until Yurri could get himself around the corner to Janice again. Janice was at Yurri's side after only a couple steps from him. She was there holding him closely wiping his face for him. "What happened back there Yurri?" she asked as soon as she had finished cleaning his face with her extra hanky.

"We won't have to worry about those specific guys anymore," he said while taking a grim look over his shoulder at where he came from. "It looks like Sixy took care of those guys for us," he said while leading her away.

Her sweet little Sixy took care of those bad men? Janice hugged Sixy to her bosom not understanding Yurri. She was very confused right now. She had the question on her face but Yurri stopped her from asking it by saying that they needed to get out of here. "We need to hide ourselves until all of this blows over. I wish that UP5 would get... Well speak of the devil."

Janice turned to look at where Yurri was looking and found that UP5 was driving up to them in a very new and fancy looking hover car. "UP5!" Janice shouted bouncing with excitement waving at the droid. "You found us!" She giggled happily as UP5 drove up to them and parked. "And you brought us another hover car to drive! And a very good looking one too!" She leaned over into the car and gave UP5 an appreciated kiss.

UP5's tentacles went stiff as boards and quivered a little when she planted that kiss. [Are you and the test subject still undamaged?] it beeped but in the translation tone it sounded a little embarrassed.

"We're fine UP5," Janice said patting one of the responsible droid's tentacle arms. "Where did you get such a nice hover car?" she asked, for it was indeed a very stylish-looking blue vehicle.

UP5 beeped sounding like a sigh. [I would rather not say,] it said sounding embarrassed again. [It looks like we have more pressing matters to attend to right now miss. I saw whole squads of those men searching in this area while I went in search of a vehicle to procure.]

That was a problem. Janice put a finger to her full lips and thought hard. What were they to do now? She looked over her shoulder at Yurri and bounced. Yurri should be able to think of something! Her handsome brave boyfriend was so smart and handsome! "Yurri!" she said bouncing up at his side. "UP5 says that there are more bad men around in this area. What do you think we should do now?" She looked up expectantly into his eyes batting those brilliant blues of hers.

Yurri had that confused look on his face, yet again. "Who told you this?" he asked.

"UP5 did you silly." Janice playfully flicked his nose. Why was Yurri being so flirty when they needed to get out of this trouble? He would get them out though. He was the one that fought those guys away from them earlier finally using his luminblade and Jai powers flinging them away for Janice to see. Her confidence in Yurri's decision making had risen profoundly since earlier this morning now that she found out and knew he was a real actual Jai.

"Wait what..." He looked at UP5. "Aww forget about it!" he said throwing up his hands. "I seriously don't want to know!" Janice gave him a cute yet baffled look that he just sighed at. He walked over to the hover car that UP5 got for them and opened a door for him and Janice. "Get in the back UP5. I'm driving."

Yurri drove them into the city proper all the while thinking of why those guys were still after them. Maybe they thought they were connected to that Jai, Rialin Epoch, somehow. The Jai was there when they jumped them in their earlier vehicle. Rialin had used the Archai to push the guys that were on Yurri away so he could get out of there. He didn't think Janice saw the Jai. Those men had only seemed concerned about getting a hold of her for some reason.

Yurri turned his head to look as they drove by one of those huge clocks on one of the city towers. It was starting to get late in the day now so Yurri planned to put them both into hiding. First, they had to disguise themselves. He had some credits on him so he believed that he could afford them suitable disguises and find them a place to stay at for tonight. They had come all the way around the city and it would take them a while to get back to their side of the city. Even with a hover car. "Hey Janice, do you know of any clothing stores we can go to that are near here so we can change our look?" he asked his girlfriend.

Janice was looking out her window now letting the wind blow her golden locks around her face looking beautiful like she normally did. He asked her again and she put her right hand on the window with her left on her forehead. *She's in deep thought now*, Yurri thought recognizing most of her body gestures by now.

After a minute of that she snapped her fingers and brought out her Trans Tablet from her purse. After turning it on and tapping it couple times, she smirked proudly at him. "Yes one of my girlfriends gave me an address to a clothing store she thought was simply fabulous. Here I have the directions in my Trans Tablet let me guide you." She gave him turn by turn directions she got from her very useful portable computer.

Yurri drove the hover car following her directions as best as he could. When they finally closed in on the store Janice squealed with glee and pointed to it. "Ohh there it is! I've always wanted to shop here. My girlfriends always get the most stylish gowns from here!" she cried happily putting her device back in her purse.

Yurri looked at the building they were headed to. It had a big sign on the front of it saying, "Welcome to 'The Galloping Gafandals'". Sounded like some weird sort of country folk dance hall to Yurri.

He parked their hover car near the exit of this establishment, in case they need to make a quick getaway. Janice had been playing with Sixy while on this drive, so she kissed it and packed her amazingly dangerous yet small pet into her majestic purse. Yurri had no idea how to break it to Janice that her newfound beloved pet was a weapon of mass *-or close to it-* destruction created by a mad scientist.

"Come on Yurri!" Janice waved to him already out of the vehicle going toward the shop.

Yurri sighed and wondered where his girlfriend got all her energy from. Right now he was beat. He looked to the UP5 droid. "UP5 you stay with the hover car until we get back." UP5 made some questioning beeps to Yurri. "I don't know. It's getting dark and we need to find a place to sleep soon. An hour or so I think we'll be in there." UP5 beeped touching the vehicle and waving an appendage over the general area. "I don't know." Yurri shrugged getting out of the hover car. "If any of those guys pop up looking for us just signal my communicator and maybe try to run them over or somethin'." UP5 gave out an affirming beep shaking its body in a semblance of a nod.

As Yurri walked up to the store called The Galloping Gafandals he hoped he had enough money on his account to pay for their hotel tonight. Nearly a fifth of his paychecks go to the dates he had with Janice; he did not have a well-paying job. He didn't think he had much left in savings.

As he reached the store door he stopped and looked back to their vehicle. Did he just have a conversation with the UP5 droid? Oh great he was talking to beeping droids like a nut job now. Janice seemed to be rubbing off on him more than he wanted. He shook his head and entered the clothing store.

He stood there and gapped as the door swung shut behind him. This wasn't any type of clothing store he'd ever been to. It was a costume shop! "Oh, there you are Yurri!" Janice said noticing Yurri turning around from looking at some materials. "Come on I think I saw just the right thing for you!" Janice grabbed his hand and pulled him along.

Yurri let himself be led by Janice as they walked through all these weird costume displays. Apparently, this was a store for humans. There were all types of body suits and lesser materials for people who wanted to look like aliens. In here were all sorts of different alien costumes all over this place. Evil looking Devlains, reptile-like Taikozens, even Gytans with big stilt boots to compensate for the height were a few that Yurri saw on his tour of this place.

As he was being led through this store, he saw a woman put on three head tentacles with fuzzy ends just like a Qwen'lynn would have on their heads. He thought he even saw those head tentacles move a little bit too, must be robotic.

Janice led them to where she thought she found them good disguises. Once there she proudly drew him up and waved a hand in front of them looking happy. Yurri looked at what Janice was showing him and frowned. "What, you don't like them?" Janice asked looking a little disheartened.

What was in front of them right now was some normal clothes you would find on any human with a baggy that had a couple bottles of various colored liquids in them and some fleshy nubs by the collar of the clothes. This didn't look like any type of disguise they could use. He told this to Janice sounding very doubtful in her choices.

"Oh they give you instructions on how to put this stuff on in the changing rooms." She pointed over to some stalls that were just down the way past more clothes. "Apparently it's becoming quite popular and chic to dress like aliens in some parts of the city. Oddly enough some alien species encourage the costume! I think they think that this way is educational for us humans to get to know other species better." She shrugged and mentioned how there must be other costume stores for aliens too to look like regular humans also. Sadly, since this was majorly a human colony, finding work if you were an alien was naturally harder than for a human. Luckily enough though people here didn't seem to care what your innards looked like if you could serve them with an approachable human smile. Mandibles, fangs, weirdly shaped eyes, and antennae basically didn't scream safe human family place.

AN ORBITING DILEMMA

"So wait," Yurri said sounding befuddled and resigned at the same time. "You have girlfriends that actually come to stores like these to dress up like they're aliens?"

"I never said that the friends I have were normal." She just winked at him, gave him a costume, and ushered him to one of the changing rooms.

He sighed heavily again as he allowed himself to be ushered into one of the changing rooms. Sighing heavily seemed to be becoming a habit of his now. Yurri tried to push away his confusing thoughts of the recent events and tried to focus on what he needed to do right now just to survive.

After Janice had Yurri in the changing room she went over to her own stall just a few steps away. She had with her an assortment of pretty dresses and skirts that came with various types of costumes for different aliens. The clothing with certain costumes was interchangeable with the various types of alien paraphernalia. This made sense because the humanoid form vastly outnumbered any other type of body form in this galaxy. After all one head, two eyes, two arms, and two legs was very common. And any tail holes, easily hidden in pants, were always made with buttons or zippers to adjust for size, if you were going to wear one of those prosthetics. Prosthetic wings were an option too but generally they were more expensive than just a simple tail. The mechanics for those were way more complex and not to mention fairly expensive too. Too pricey for attachments that were only for looks really. Not useful for anything else.

Janice started to get undressed and looked through the costumes picked to see which to try on first. "Hello miss," a feminine voice said to her. "Would you like help or instructions on how those particular costumes are put on?"

"No I'm fine but thanks," Janice answered. "My girlfriends already told me how this works." She continued putting the costume on zipping her back down and thought that it was so good of the owners of this store to have installed computer/droid helpers to tell and help people with how to put this stuff on. Maybe she should have told Yurri about the robotic helpers.

"AAAAHHCK!!!" a cry came from the stall a little way from Janice's. It sounded like Yurri!

"Yurri are you all right?" Janice called out.

"Crap no! This stall has arms! And it tried to get my clothes grabbing at me!"

Janice put a hand on her mouth trying to stifle some laughter. She really *should* have told Yurri about those. "Yurri those are 'helping hands'. Some of the costumes here are so complicated and difficult to get on these are here to help people get the stuff on or to instruct them how to. Just let yourself be guided by the droid voice helper and put that stuff on. I think disguising ourselves like aliens would be better than simply changing our clothes, don't you?" She heard him sigh, yet again; she's going to have to talk to him about that, as he mumbled that he would go along with this.

Janice smiled as she pulled her skirt over her head. Yurri was becoming so delightful to be around. Though his constitution was a bit weak considering how easy it was to put him down with just a kiss. This flaw of his was surprisingly endearing though. As the dress came over her head something dropped out of one of her pockets. She bent down to see what she dropped, and oh… it was the ring Yurri had proposed with back in that farm mansion. She held it out in front of her inspecting it. She looked at it and saw that it changed color depending on how it was struck by the light.

"Princess?" said a quite small feminine voice coming from the top of Janice's head.

"Oh!" Janice jumped dropping the ring. "Don't scare me like that Décore!" she angrily whispered to her droid. She bent down to retrieve her ring.

"What's going on princess? I can feel your emotions going all jumbly."

Oh that's right. Décore doesn't have eyes in her current form. She does have excellent hearing enough to make a person think she had ocular input in that form though, thanks to her father's brilliant programming of course. As she thought about what to tell Décore Janice heard someone talking to Yurri. Apparently, somebody had come to check out why someone had screamed.

"I don't know," she said as she stripped off more clothing. "It's Yurri. And I think I'm actually starting to fall in love with him."

"I thought your feelings for him were only superficial."

Janice sighed quietly searching through her feelings again. "I thought so too, but after what's been happening to us today, I'm finding him quite gallant, thoughtful, and very heroic at times. Also back at that farming house I think Yurri proposed to me."

"He did what?!" Décore shouted that whisper. Décore always insisted to communicate vocally with Janice never using the translation feature for just talking to her.

"Shhh!" Janice listened to the conversation between Yurri and the worker in this store to see if they heard. They were talking about good hotels near here. He was so responsible. "At the farming house he gave me this ring," Janice said holding it up for Décore to see rolling it around. Janice heard a little whirring from Décore as she formed an eye from one of her hair prongs so she could look at the ring.

"Ooh, that *is* pretty!" the girl heard her hair decoration say. "He even had it made in a way that it shows all your favorite colors too!"

"Yes," Janice replied slipping the ring onto the proper finger admiring at how well it fit and marveled how pretty it was. He must have taken a lot of time to have it made this way. How *did* he get her ring size anyways? "I hope Yurri realizes the position he's put me into. I am on the run from my parents after all and I don't want to get married now. They might find me because of it!"

"Wait," Décore said sounding like she had a brilliant idea. "If you married Yurri you wouldn't have to marry that old fat goat your mother set you up with!"

That was right... Janice tapped her chin in thought. Maybe it was just the blond in her, but she was really coming to like Yurri being a Jai and all. It was just that... Oh she didn't know! She shook her head vigorously and threw her arms down. Was this how her mother felt when she fell for a commoner like her father? She knew her mother had infuriated her grandparents. She had to think clearly about this. Maybe Yurri hadn't actually proposed to her. Maybe Yurri had just stumbled while looking at an exotic ring in that display room. Maybe Yurri really wasn't a Jai at all with Ron being the idiot he was thought that any boyfriend of Janice's would have to be a Jai and Yurri had only found that luminblade by accident in that display room also. And maybe she should just break up with him to save him from any harm from those men that were obviously after her and go home. Oh how she wished her uncle Dism were here! He always gave such good advice on problems like these.

She took off the ring to inspect it again and noticed the engraving it had on the inseam of it. It said, "For Jan, my special girl". Oh that tears it. This really was a proposal ring and Yurri really was a Jai. It fit her finger perfectly, it showed all her favorite colors in such an amazing way, and it had this inscription in it too. What was she going to do? She stuck it in a special spot in her purse and thought to ignore Yurri's proposal until she figured out what to do with him. Though coming up to her mother and telling her that she was going to have Jai grand-babies would certainly curb her mother's anger at Janice.

As Janice got the costume all the way on, she told Décore what was engraved on the ring. Her droid was delighted in this! Décore thought that she should marry Yurri and end the stress with her parents and go home. The little decoration droid had been complaining of not being able to chat with new droid friends and people ever since Janice ran away from home. "No, Décore, I can't..." Janice said sounding very unsure about this decision herself.

"Why not?"

Ugh! Décore was so impertinent at times. She had the gown fully on by now and was looking at her reflection in the mirror. "How do you think this dress makes me look?"

"You're avoiding the question, princess." Janice gave out an exasperated sigh looking up. "Just give me one good reason and I'll drop this completely," Décore promised.

"Décore shut up or I'll turn off your vocal units," Janice said in a smooth serious tone. She didn't want to talk about this right now. She angrily applied the yellow skin dye to her skin to make it look purple. As she applied the dye solve the dying color had a rippling effect on her skin. One drop of this stuff on her skin and it blossomed out in a circle that kept getting bigger covering the area of her skin ten times larger than the original drop. The brown dye reversed the effect covering an even larger area with one drop. She meticulously applied the ointment to all the visible areas of her body. She was not avoiding Décore's question because she didn't know herself. She had come to really like Yurri within these past hours during this day and to enjoy his cunning and bravery. It was merely that a person always needs more time to think some things through properly. Maybe she should think through all of this as a brunette.

Décore kept herself silent as Janice finished with the last parts of the costume, putting on the neck piece that came with it. The aliens they were disguising themselves as were called Ackers. They come from a weird planet with shifting winds that dramatically change the atmosphere. The thing around their necks was somewhat like having a second set of nostrils. They breathe in both oxygen and whatever else it was that they breathe in. Janice thinks she remembers that the cause of the chaotic shifting atmosphere was because of the instability of the planet's core. For some reason, Janice didn't know, the core continually sucked in the atmosphere and released very erratic amounts of different types of gas.

Janice finished changing and smiled at herself in the mirror. The neck application was designed to match the current subject's skin tone to complete the effect. She turned herself around in front of the mirror again. The clothing that came with this particular type of costume wasn't too stylish, so Janice stripped herself again putting on a different set of clothes to try on to see how they looked on her.

When she finally found the one she liked she pressed the button to the device on her back to register these garments to the PC2. It was blue and green with loose shoulders on it with lacey purple frills at the ends of the skirt which ended just above her knees and a high decent neckline. That was one of the ingenious things that the device she got from Tom Finny. It was small and fit comfortably in between a person's shoulder blades. You only needed to press it and think what you wanted it to do. It was very advanced technology. From what Janice knows about Mr. Tom's company they always come up with things like this. They have been approached by the military a couple times, but the military has always been denied this type of neural detection. There already was a type of neural detection out there but you had to get some serious hardware installed into your spinal cord and cerebellum before it worked. A very painful and uncomfortable procedure to go through and way to be afterwards, it was simply a lot cheaper to train people to push buttons with controls than do it the expensive way.

Based on what Janice had heard from her friends on how to work this device properly a person merely needs to attach a general emotion and feeling to certain type clothing and think about how the garment makes you feel and push the button on it to have that particular clothing summoned back to your body. She didn't know the technicalities of all that but that was the way with most people and things like this.

Ok, she had the dress on she wanted to buy with the other costume accessories on right now, but she noticed her other gown on the floor. Oh that was right she wanted to keep that in the PC2 too. "Janice?" a knock came from the stall's door. "Are you nearly done yet?" It was Yurri and he was apparently already done with dressing up.

"Almost, I only need to set a few things straight first and dye my hair," Janice answered. She then imagined herself down into her skippies pressing that button, —*It was silly not to do this before but old habits were hard to get around*— donned her brown and blue dress again, slipped back on her shoes, the PC2 doesn't work with shoes either from what she's heard, took out another bottle from that baggie, quickly dyed her blond hair pink, and came out to meet Yurri with the price tag of the garment she picked in her hands. She wasn't a thief after all and she could merely leave the other clothes in here. Some attendants would get them later.

When Janice left her changing stall, she saw that Yurri had donned all the costume materials properly and looked like a handsome green haired Acker. He had decided to dress himself mostly with the clothes he had on before choosing to leave the garments that came with the other costume materials in the changing room. He chose a dapper looking deep green sleeveless vest to have on over his regular shirt. "Huh," he said looking her up and down in a way she found herself beginning to appreciate. "I thought you took a couple more clothing sets in there with you. Didn't find anything you liked?" There were a couple people coming in and out of the changing stalls now but otherwise they were mostly alone.

Janice looked down on herself and saw that she was in her original outfit. "Oh that's all right Yurri. I have the one I chose set up with my PC2 device with a couple other sets of clothing that nice mad scientist gave me," she smiled at him.

"I might regret asking this but what is a PC2? I've never heard of it before and I have no idea what it even does."

She smiled at him giggling a little bit with her hand on her mouth. He was so quaint at times and for some reason she found that blatantly attractive. "PC2 is short for Portable Closet version two. I think you can only find these devices in our solar system, but it is catching on to other systems too, I think. These devices allow a person to switch what they're wearing with another gown or suit or something that has been registered to the device previously. I've heard that this device can break down the molecules of clothing into a digital format and switch the person's clothing to another one altogether. The more complex and harder a material is the more impossible it is to put the material in the device. So simply put living organic and or robotic material is out of the question." She shrugged but proud of herself for giving such comprehensive explanations whilst a blonde. Well, she had dyed her hair pink, but she told Décore to keep her hair blond. As long as she knew her droid was keeping her hair the proper color, she didn't think it would affect her personality in any way though she had no idea how she would act with such an unnatural color for a human.

"Whoa," Yurri said giving her a doubtful look. "That sounds more like science fiction to me, but I can't honestly say that I know of everything in this galaxy."

"Here, want to see how it works?" Yurri gave her that skeptical look again but nodded his head. "Ok I'll switch to that wonderful dancing gown that you liked so much when we were at Mr. Finny's place." As she looked down the small hallway to better concentrate on the change, she reached back to touch her PC2. Her Jai boyfriend looked sick though he still looked like he was rooting her on.

This was the first time she had actually used the PC2 to switch in-between clothing after leaving Tom's place, she was so excited in getting this device her mind didn't notice anything out of place at all, and it didn't happen the way she thought it would. First of all her girlfriends had told her with these things there was always a colored orbed flash for a second for some reason. She felt her clothing shift from being her stylish skirt and blossom into that wonderful dancing gown she found in Mr. Tom's huge closet. Janice looked down on herself when the switch was complete and smiled. Again she was in that wonderful white dancing ballroom dress that she got such a strange and intense reaction before from Yurri. It wasn't like she was asking him to marry her or anything, this was for dancing. She looked up to see Yurri's reaction.

She found him on the ground moaning like someone had just slugged him in the face. "Yurri are you okay?!" she asked rushing up to his side worriedly. He groaned as she helped him stand up again. She noticed that his nose was bleeding, so she pressed a hanky, from her purse, up to it for him. He groaned again as he took hold of the hanky with his eyes squeezed shut. "Yurri what happened?" Janice asked with serious worry on her voice. Why did he have his eyes shut?

"I'll tell you but first are you decent?" he said looking like he was avoiding looking at her with his eyes still shut.

"Yes I am. I have that dress on now." Did he get hit in the head really hard or something?

He opened his eyes and sighed in relief looking at her. "How do those devices change a person's clothing without making a person look bare?"

Janice, still confused, wondered about this strange question. "From what I've heard from my girlfriends the device is supposed to give you a colored bright orbed light around you between switches... Ohh!" she exclaimed fully understanding Yurri's question now putting her hand to her mouth. The device first had to redigitize the clothing a person was wearing, putting it back into its internal memory, then it placed the selected clothing on the person's body though this process did take a couple seconds. Janice remembered that when she switched clothing there wasn't a colored bright orbed flash as they switched. That flash was supposed to screen anyone looking at them from the changes in clothing without hurting anyone's eyes or seeing anyone bare. If the orbed flash didn't go off what did Yurri see?

"Yurri?" she asked blushing like suns going super nova with her hands still on her face not looking at him. "Did you see me... completely bare?" She would find this out and then go somewhere to die quietly.

"No, I don't think I could have survived something like that," he laughed weakly. "But for just an instant you were in nothing but your underwear which floored me." He put a comforting hand on her shoulder at a respectful distance away. "I don't think you should be using that device anywhere a lot of people are. Professor Tom did tell us that this device is a prototype to what he has out now."

Oh Yurri was such a proper, kind, and decent man. She should figure out a way to reward him for all his chivalrous actions. She took a couple calming breaths to gather herself. Some men were coming out of some other changing rooms looking like full-fledged aliens now. This place certainly was popular.

"Yurri?" she asked tentatively bringing her hands down from her face calmly placing them by her hips. "What do you think we should do now? It is getting late and we need to find a place to sleep."

"Well first off we need to pay for these costumes and hope that having these will throw them off our trail," he said that while looking a little grim with the hanky she gave him for his bloody nose at his side now. She thought it was the same one he lent to her earlier that day and it also looked a little more bloodied too. Yup that's the same hanky she used on his nose earlier when she met up with him at the farm mansion.

"What are we going to do after that?" she asked him getting a little impatient with him stating the obvious.

"We need to find a place to sleep. Though in all honesty I'm not sure I'll have enough money for a room. I took a look at these price tags and this stuff is pretty expensive. I might have to make a couple calls to ask for some favors." He grimaced as he said that.

Was that all? She could very easily purchase all these items of course. She had been planning to be away for special trips for quite a while. She had a habit of doing exactly that, saving up money and putting it away into a secret account where she could access it later just in case while away from her parents. Janice had an account with a big king's ransom in it. "Oh you don't have to worry about the price of anything. I'll pay for all of it," she said while lovingly patting his face. "You've done so much for us already. I feel it my duty to pitch in somewhat with all of this," she said pressing herself closer to Yurri while caressing his attractive features. When had he become so handsome? It must be that eye-catching color of his skin now. There were more men going in and out those stalls as they talked to each other. Some of them were talking by one of those stalls.

Yurri grabbed her hand, pushing it away from his face, and took a few steps back giving her a quizzical look. "Are you ok Jan? You're acting a little... weird."

She was acting weird? What was he talking about? She only did things that felt right. "We can talk about this later cutie. Right now we have to get ourselves snuggled away for the night." Her stomach growled at her reminding her that she hasn't had anything to eat since brunch this morning, and they were interrupted in the middle of that too. "And find something to eat too." She blushed patting her stomach. Yurri whole heartedly agreed to that too.

They started walking over to the front counter to buy what they got. It looked like the store was about to close so there were a lot of people around for last minute shopping. While walking to the checkout desk Janice remembered she needed to have on the dress she's going to buy on so in the middle of their walk she reached to press the button on the device on her back. "No wait Janice!"

Yurri drove their hover car to the nearest hotel he could find. He hoped they could order some food at the inn too. The sun was setting by this time in the west of the city. Yurri had asked if UP5 knew of any hotels that had a dining hall in them too. UP5 beeped and pointed Yurri the way to the nearest hotel UP5 had on its internal maps. Yurri knew it was extremely bizarre for him to be able to kind of understand what the droid was saying. Nothing this past day was making sense to him anymore. With all the strange people he's been meeting and all those whacky and disturbing events his girlfriend and him have been going through he was not entirely sure he was still completely sane. Yurri took all of this stoically wondering which all mighty being he ticked off to have them start throwing all of these crazy events at him.

As they traveled, he couldn't help but notice that Janice was starting to act very weird herself. Still like a blond but even more so. Acting very distracted she was sitting next to him in the car playing with Sixy again. Was it just him or was she getting a little more childish as he drove on? She also kept on petting his head and randomly jumping up to point at something she found delightful all the while pressing her wonderfully soft self onto Yurri in a very seductive and yet equally uncomfortable way, weird combination.

The terrain of what Yurri drove through was familiar enough for him. He had driven into downtown enough in the past, well generally enough anyways. The owner of the restaurant where he worked was a little shady. An old friend of his parents but still the man acted shady. He kept on having Yurri drive into town to fetch "special" ingredients to put in the food they make. Of course Yurri already knew why he acted so secretive about this in the first place. The man had ordered ingredients for food from planets that weren't all that friendly about sharing the plants, produce and livestock only found on their planets. Something about supply and demand or something like that anyways, the underworld of food marketing Yurri thought.

He pulled up their hover car into the parking lot of the hotel that UP5 had directed him to. He parked, not really caring where, and eagerly made his way into the hotel not noticing or even really caring about the layout of the place. He was getting dead tired through this heinous day. UP5 went in the direction where personal droids of people who stayed here went. Yurri had asked UP5 to direct them to a hotel that had some security so they could be sure to sleep in peace tonight. By now Yurri had obtained UP5's frequency number so he could get a hold of the droid in the morning or whenever.

After going through the front hotel doors heading into the hotel Yurri was stopped when Janice came up to him and pleasantly, in an uncomfortable way, bumped into him. "Yurri you go in and get something to eat in the dining hall," she said while patting his face. "I'll handle the arrangements for our room, and I'll find you later in the café. You've been worked hard enough as it is my brave handsome Jai man and you deserve a rest!" She enticingly brushed herself up against Yurri one last time kissing him on the cheek then went up to the front desk.

What the frell was going on with Janice? She never acted this familiar with him before. Yurri shook his head again like he has done so many times before thinking that maybe Janice had some clothing on too tight somewhere or she was a little tipsy. Though he has been with her all day and they haven't had anything to eat or drink since this morning. Maybe it had to do something with the color of her hair being pink.

Yurri stopped in mid-step at that notion. He shook his head in the middle of the decorated halls of the inn as other patrons of the hotel mingled around. Where did that thought come from? People's personalities don't change with the color of a person's hair. Or did they? A dislodged memory of Janice passionately kissing him while she was a black-haired vixen popped into his head. Now where did that come from?

Poor Yurri shook his head thinking it has been a very long and stressful day today. He quickly found his way to the café being led by the customer hotel maps he found in the orange carpeted halls. In the café Yurri smiled when he found out that they were having a buffet for all their customers

AN ORBITING DILEMMA

today. He grabbed a couple trays for himself and Janice and quickly filled them up with various types of cheeses, fruits, and vegetables with a variety of specially cooked meats. He was pretty proud of himself for the setup of food he prepared for himself and Janice.

After saying a quick prayer of thanks at the table he sat down in he dug in. The café was full of dwindling customers. People were starting to go to their rooms for bed. Yurri had overstuffed each tray and was happily draining one of its contents when Janice finally arrived. She sat down but moved her chair closer to Yurri, so they were both touching each other they were so close. This made it hard for Yurri to eat without bumping Janice in uncomfortable spots. Janice came up with a solution to this problem. In where she was the one who was feeding Yurri. At first, he protested and said she should eat her fill first before trying to help him. Though she did object enough to this to the point where he thought she was going to stab him with her fork. So he stoically took it and let her feed him and herself. She *was* acting very weird. In a fuzzy touchy feely kill you if she doesn't get what she wants type of psychotic way.

Once they were done eating, and Janice paid their tab, -*Where did Jan get all this money? He didn't even know if she had a job or not.*- they went to the room that Janice set up for them. In a strange way, that didn't surprise Yurri too much, he found them in a suite for newlyweds. Before Janice could set herself up to go to bed Yurri ran into the bathroom saying that he might be in there for a couple hours. He gave her the excuse of having the runs. She pouted at this while sitting on the king-sized bed.

Yurri stayed in the bathroom for a complete hour until he thought that Janice finally went to sleep. While in there he changed into some complimentary brown pajamas he found in there. He tentatively peeked his head out the bathroom door and saw that she was in bed breathing in a smooth slow rhythm under the bed covers. Ach, he was so tired that he felt like he could sleep on pointy rocks. Instead of that uncomfortable sleeping position Yurri settled for grabbing a couple cushions out of a few love seats, that were not big enough for one person to lie on and settled himself down for sleeping on the floor by the door.

At first through the night he shifted on the floor as he slept having dreams where Ron was chasing him wielding a man-sized foot intending to use it to club him to death with that crazy scientist clinging on it seeming to be grossly sucking on that foot too. Those hideous alien females that had chased him and Janice before somehow had shrunk down, gotten on top of his head, were dancing, and twining themselves into his hair in a weirdly disgusting erotic dance. To top it off Janice was there running beside him, her hair changing color erratically, and with Sixy in her arms that every now and then jumped off Janice and devoured entire sections of the city's population. The extremely weird and disturbing dreams ran through Yurri's mind through most of the night.

After shifting restlessly through most of this night Yurri found that he was beginning to have more pleasant and soothing dreams late in the night. The pleasant aroma of special flowers and fruits filled his nostrils, just like the perfume Janice always wears which led him into even more pleasant dreams. For some reason he felt more comfortable too as if he weren't sleeping on the floor anymore. It was as if he were lying on a warm comfortable fluffy pillow.

After that fitful night of sleep Yurri woke up but kept his eyes closed relishing the comfortable way arms were wrapped around him. Wait what? Those weren't his arms! He opened his eyes to get a surprise of his life. He was now lying next to Janice in that king-sized bed! How did he get up here?!

Janice yawned, stretching out moving her arms away, making Yurri very quickly and quite noisily jump out of the bed checking his person to make sure he still had his clothes on. Thankfully he did. Janice sat up and looked at him in a way that made him feel very uncomfortable. After all he was raised with high standards from his parents, which he took into the very center of his being. "Ok what happened last night?" he asked that very direct question looking at Janice his face afire.

"Oh nothing much," Janice said stretching enticingly. Her shoulders were bare except for the straps that were over them. One strap fell loose as she stretched her arms down. Somewhere she had gotten a red silky night gown. Janice adjusted that strap giving Yurri a mischievous smile. And for some reason she still had that weird decoration in her hair. "You just looked so uncomfortable and distressed lying there on the floor I thought my brave cuddly handsome Jai would sleep better if he slept on this wonderful bed here with me," she said while caressing the spot on the bed where he had been. "So I picked you up and tucked you in."

She was giving him that alluring smile again. "Janice, I don't know how you do things on your home planet," Yurri said while stressfully raking a hand through his colored hair. Heck he didn't even know where her home planet was. He has heard her reading to herself some news from an unknown planet to him, maybe that was her planet, but other than that he knew nothing about her origins. "But we're not even married and shouldn't be doing things like this!" He blushed furiously thinking of how he would be able to explain this to his dad. Forget his dad, how would he explain this to his Mom?! He would rather face a thousand years in the belly of a demonic pit monster Kaleras than face his mother about this!!!

"Not married *yet* anyways," she laughed with her hand to her mouth. "Oh don't worry you old fuddy duddy," she giggled waving a hand at him. "Nothing happened. I only picked you up and tucked you in."

Huh? "Hang on a second…" Yurri blanched. "You *picked* me up?" And what did she mean by "Not married yet"?

"There are some things you don't know about me that I am reconsidering in whether to tell you or not." She winked at him, hinting at the unknown.

"Ok that does it!" a loud female voice called out of nowhere. Janice swatted at her hair decoration yelling at it but surprisingly it jumped away and transformed itself into a spider-like form. "No mistress! I won't allow you to do something like what you were thinking about doing!" the decoration shouted at Janice.

"Décore not here! I command you to return to your proper form at your proper place right now!!" Janice shouted at her disobedient hair decoration.

What the frelling crap?! What the freck was going on?! Yurri stood there with his mouth opened as Janice and her hair decoration argued at each other, just like his younger sisters did when he was back at home, her decoration dodging her grabs. He watched this unharmonious triad until Janice had noticed him staring. She at least had the decency to blush.

"You need to tell this man everything mistress," Janice's weird robotic hair decoration said while on the night table by the bed. "You have endangered his life with those men after you now. Tell Yurri right now or I will!" To top this spectacle off the now spider droid folded its front forelegs looking like crossed arms.

"Okay! Okay!" Janice exclaimed throwing her arms up in the kneeling position she was in on the bed. "Yurri, sweetie," she said while putting her feet on the floor and standing up. "There are a couple things you need to know about me."

"You bet there is!"

"Shut up Décore! Don't make me turn off your reasoning software..." Janice gave her small droid a good glare down before she turned to look at Yurri and smiled worriedly. "You might want to sit down for this hon. Also let me order us some food to come up here too. I don't think what I'm going to share with you will be very agreeable."

She used the in-room phone to call for some room service up and then sat on a side of the bed patting her hand on it to encourage Yurri to join her. She was so cool, calm, and collected. The young man had never seen his girlfriend act this way before. He stood there staring at her not knowing how to properly react to this insane situation. After a couple moments of silence Janice broke down into sobbing fits covering her face with her hands.

Oop, Yurri hated to see women cry, especially when he was the cause of it. He came over to Janice's side, sat on the bed with her, put an arm around her, and hugged her. This was the only way he knew how to get a woman to stop from crying, and it usually worked.

"You're so good to me my Yurri!" she cried leaning very much into Yurri's side crying onto his shoulder. After which she relayed her story to him through fits and sobs. She told him the story how she escaped her parents years ago, it was quite ingenious how she did that and Yurri was impressed. She then related the few years she ran about the galaxy avoiding her parents, he found out that she had stashed away lots of money for this excursion, how she was a princess third in line for the throne, how she met Ron at the place she had been currently hiding, and the few things that happened while there. She had only decided to become a blond full time after a few close encounters with the people that were sent by her parents to find her nearly found her. Her story was interrupted by room service arriving. Yurri stood up, went to the door to answer it, and mechanically brought the food to the dining table that was in the room.

Janice had herself more composed by this time and was wiping her eyes with the bed sheet. She came over to Yurri's side sitting down at the dining table. He instinctively set the table with the food he had and sat down. Janice wiped some oddly colored bangs from her face as she wiped the last of her tears away. For some reason her hair looked like pink-tinted glass. Yurri was feeling very numb throughout his entire body from what Janice was able to share with him about herself. From what she's told him so far this was because her hair decoration, Décore, wasn't on her head at the moment. "And that is how I came to this planet Yurri. I hope you don't think any less of me." She gave him a look that told him he would break her if he did.

"And ha," she laughed weakly trying to compose herself. "It looks like my dad's assumption of my hair somehow electrochemically signals my brain which color it is at the moment was right," she looked away from Yurri to the window, "proves that my personality changes even if I don't know my hair color at the moment," she rambled again as when as she gets nervous, holding her left shoulder.

They sat there and quietly ate their breakfast together after saying a quick reflexive prayer of thanks. It was the same type of food that they had eaten for supper last night only in breakfast format, still good though. The chefs here must like fixing their food in a special way to mark it in the customers' minds. "So your real full name is Janiece Agra?" Janice nodded her head as she wiped her mouth with a napkin. "Seriously I don't think that was a very good cover name at all for you. I honestly can't see the difference between that and Janice." Right now Yurri was trying to break the insufferable awkwardness of this situation. He did have talent at breaking insufferable awkwardness. So he thought to simply tick off Janice or Janiece or whatever her name was to keep her from crying again. He would figure out how he felt about this new information later.

"I was a blond at the time when I thought up my cover name," she defended herself in a mildly affronted way. She now had Décore on her head, she had put on the droid decoration while they were eating, and it was making her hair into a weird pink brownish blend. She also sounded like she was having an easier time constructing her sentences and thoughts too now.

"Still, changing it to Janice from Janiece, I personally thought you were smarter as a blond."

Now that got her riled up and not so weepy anymore, sometimes Yurri was too good at defusing situations and making them into the exact opposite of what they were. "I was a dumb blond when I thought that up! I'm stupid as a blond! If you haven't noticed I'm not all up there when I'm like that!" She had finished her plate by this time. She stood up with her tray to put it down the disposal unit in the room. She indignantly stood by Yurri while he finished with her hands on her ample hips.

"And you named experiment 666 Sixy. Why?" playing dumb he asked that looking up at her while shoveling more food into his mouth. This tactic seemed to be working. He would rather have a ticked off woman sharing the same room with him instead of a weepy one. Even if he had to dodge some throws.

"My hair was translucent at the time and I'm very child-like in those situations," she harrumphed at him as he took another bite. Yurri had a particular tone in his voice when he ever did this and with most people this same tone just annoyed them to no ends. When coupled with what he was doing right now it had a significant effect at aggravating his intended target.

"I don't even know how you can let your personality be dictated by the color of your hair. Maybe your mom ate something weird the day you were conceived. Royal people are always eating odd things."

"Are you implying that my family is weird?" Janice asked in a huff with her arms folded under her bosom.

"Yes and no," he replied. Janice cocked her head in confusion. "Everybody has their own weird family quirks in their own way. It really depends on how you look at things. But people with royal lineage—-now that's a whole different story. Most royals are stupid and ignorant of 'common' people's worries."

"Like me?" Janice sniffed in an affronted way.

"No, not like you." Yurri finished his meal, wiping his face with a napkin as he stood up to look at Janice. "I always thought royal people were snobs and dumber than a dead asteroid worm. But you are far smarter than I ever expected." By now Yurri's memories of the incident before where Janice had kissed him for the first time had been fully revived and compiled in his mind again. And at least now he knew how she could speak to animals like that. A weird princess power…

"I never have been smart as a blonde! I'm only smart with dresses and makeup and things like that!" She stamped her foot sounding like she was pouting now.

"Were you one hundred percent blonde all the time since you've been on this planet?" His method was working.

"Yes I didn't dare change my hair color for fear of my parents finding me here! It was torturous for me to be a dumb blond for all those months!" Janice threw up her hands looking red in the face. "My parents both know that I vehemently despise being a blond. So, as I've said before, I'm disguising myself with blond hair. They know I would never willingly become a brain-dead blond!"

"You couldn't have been that dumb of a blond. As I think I remember you know more about this planet than I do. What were those insects called again, leichers maybe?"

"No they were called lintches, you insufferable man!" his girlfriend said folding her arms under her chest again sounding exasperated. Now Yurri was actually coming to like this side of Janice.

"Ah," he shrugged receiving a glower from the woman. "It doesn't matter what they're called. What matters to me is that, even though a blond at the time, you instinctively searched out information that would be useful to you in the future. I've been living here about four times longer than you and I had no idea about those nasty things. Therefore, you are one smart cookie even as a blond!" He pointed at her smirking.

"Oh! Oh! Oh!" Janice exclaimed in frustration slapping her hands to her sides. "You… you man!!" She lunged at him pulling his head down for a long-wet exhilarating kiss.

It was a good thing that the bed was behind Yurri for he fell straight back once his tormentor released him.

"Was it really necessary to knock him out like that again, princess?" the voice on top of Janiece's head asked.

Princess Janiece shook her head thoughtfully at the moment. Maybe it hadn't been very necessary to put Yurri down like that again, but it had been very satisfying. She had washed the pink out her hair and had used Décore to turn her hair purple a color that she knew this species of aliens to have in their usual hair colors. Janiece was a little surprised that Décore could do such a color. She had left Yurri unconscious on the bed for about an hour or so it seemed. She thought the extra nap time would do him good for all the stress she's been putting him through anyways. That was enough time for her to take a shower and get cleaned up in the bathroom. She seemed to be able to think far more clearly with purple hair than with pink. Now that she thinks about it, she thought her mind was clearer more as a blond than as a pink head. Along with washing herself she had smartly washed all their dirty clothes too. After taking their things out of the in room small clothes washer and drier she packed everything away properly. Including the extra hanky she had on her. It had gotten pretty bloody with its use.

"You heard what he was saying to me. He was trying to make me angry!" Janiece said angrily packing up her purse with her now clean and dry but worn handkerchief.

"Yes, I heard, and he was trying to convince you that you aren't as stupid as you thought when you're a blond. I don't know why that would make you angry with him though."

"It made me angry because he was getting the better of me!" she huffed. She went to the opened window in their room and looked for Sixy. They were on the ground level of the hotel so Janiece had let her little pet outside through it so he could do his business. She had paid a little extra for the accommodation of being able to pick out their room after all.

"And so in doing that he deserved to be knocked out flat again even though he was complementing you while winning that argument?"

"On both counts!" Janiece said harshly. "I wanted him to shut up for winning that argument, but I also wanted to thank him for his weirdly kind words too," she finished softly. She caught her small dangerous pet as it leaped up to the window and brought it inside with her. After a quick peek outside it looked like Sixy had behaved himself out there. She knew he wouldn't misbehave around her. "Yurri is too decent for his own good sometimes." She placed Sixy on her shoulders and the fuzzy cute little thing wrapped itself around her neck in a very comfortable way. She petted Sixy's head.

"I think I could also do that color for you if you wanted," Décore mused. "Well at least we know now that you should never have pink hair."

Janiece didn't know about that... She looked to the bathroom where Yurri was at the moment taking his own shower and getting ready for the day. She had changed herself into a long divided white skirt that had lovely light pink stars over across her shoulders and chest that she had obtained from Mr. Finny. While she had pink hair, she could think of nothing except amorous thoughts. Some of those thoughts made the princess blush when she remembered them but maybe it would be fun to try out the pink hair with Yurri after they get married.

Wait... she rubbed her temples, was she really truly coming to love him that much? Did she truly believe that he had Jai powers now? She thought she did. Or maybe that had been the blond in her at that time. She did see him use Archai powers after all, but still there was something itching the back of her mind about that subject, maybe not. It wasn't all that important to her now she realized. Besides she knew Yurri to be a terrible liar. She decided to let things fully unfurl before making any life-changing decisions like that.

She heard Yurri shut off the shower. "Hey Jan," he called from inside the bathroom, "have you seen my clothes around here somewhere?"

Janiece smiled when she heard this. She had been planning for this. She had quietly snatched his dirty rags away while he was behind that opaque shower door. "I have some clothes for you right here, Yurri." He stuck an arm out the door and she handed him the set of clothes she picked out for him. He pulled them in and shut the door.

"Uhh Janice these aren't my clothes," Yurri said from behind the door.

She giggled mischievously. "I think you would look more dashing in that. While you were asleep and showering, I took a quick tour of this hotel and had our dirty clothes washed. They have a mini mall built right in near the entrance to this place. I saw what I gave you and thought you would look so handsome in those. More official, I think. You are a Jai after all, and I've always wanted to dress a Jai." Months ago she had already obtained his sizes to allow her to more adequately dress him if she so chooses. She could hear him sigh through the bathroom door. He's really been doing that a lot lately.

"Janice I really need to tell you something."

"Wait until you've changed into those clothes! I really want to see how you look!" He grunted in compliance in a way that said, "This is it".

He came out of the bathroom with a peculiar grim look on his face. He had put on what she gave him though. It had a long dark brown coat with it with tails that brushed the back of his thighs. He had on a wrist-length jacket which emphasized his nicely round, large, and firm arms. He had to do a lot of heavy lifting for his job from what Janiece understood about where he worked. Lots of heavy platters of food or something like that. This coat nicely matched his black pants with various pockets throughout it, which she knew he favored.

"Oh." Janiece hopped up to his side straightening his clothes for him. "You look so handsome and striking in those Yurri! All you need now is your luminblade." She hopped away from him with one of his arms outstretched grasping air with that grim look still on his face. She came back to him happily carrying his luminblade. "Now we just clip this on your belt." She clipped it on for him and stepped back looking him up and down. "There, you look very dashing and quite official now."

She continued on even though her boyfriend looked like he wanted to say something. "I think we should try to figure out how to get to the star port on the eastern edge of the city where I have my ship. Once we get into my ship, we can go to Tyy and lie low for a while. I think my parents would slack off on the marriage they planned for me if I introduced them to my Jai boyfriend." Janiece was very proud of herself for coming up with that exceptional plan. It solved so many of her problems at once. And while a blonde she had always let others do the planning for her. She always got headaches thinking too much as a blonde.

"Janice I… Wait, you found your spaceship keys? I thought you lost those." Apparently, he had a good memory too.

"Yes I found them deep in my purse. I really need to clean this thing out and organize everything in it. I know it has some self-defense tools that my dad made for me in here somewhere," she said as she absent-mindedly investigated the contents of her quizzical carry-on luggage that was her purse.

"Janice, we need to talk."

"Oh you don't have to call me Janice anymore. Just call me by my real name, Janiece," she said waving at him while still searching through her purse.

"Wait what?" he said while putting a hand on his forehead giving her an odd look. "What does it even matter if I call you Janice or Janiece? It's the same *frickin'* name! It even sounds the same!"

Ignoring his unacceptable use of expletives the more than proper princess answered her boyfriend. "It's my proper name. And the difference is in the pronunciation. You would say nice at the end of Ja*nice* and niece at the end of Ja*niece*. Oh if it bugs you so much you still can call me Janice. I'll even think of myself as Janice. I like that name. Makes me feel like a rebel." She stuck her tongue out and winked at him. She was having such fun with this hair color! Maybe she should explore the full color spectrum and see how she acts with each color. How would she act with blue or green in her hair or maybe even plaid, if that was even probable? Oh the possibilities!

"DhaHAH!" Yurri cried throwing his hands up. "Whatever! I need to tell you something important Jan! I'm not really a Jai! I have no idea why Ron even thought I was one! I found this luminblade in that farming mansion too! There, now you know… What's so funny?"

Janice had a hand on her lips holding back laughter. She thought she had already figured that little secret out about Yurri. She was a very smart girl after all. Once she wasn't under the blond or pink influence anyways. She merely liked playing on with the façade. She was still thinking about certain possibilities though. Certain possibilities that didn't displease her as much as she thought they would when she could think clearer. So she thought to leave herself ignorant to certain facts to see how all this played out in the end. This was fun!

"Yurri, only a blonde would think you were a composed, dynamic, and impressive Jai. I thought to just play along in the fantasy a little longer." She continued to giggle behind her hand waving her other hand at him.

"Oh okay. That makes me feel better… I think." He cocked his head, looking at her as if not entirely sure he enjoyed his girlfriend's reaction to this.

"We've only known each other under a year now. Let's get to know each other better when we get to my home planet." She playfully cat pawed his shoulder. "I'm sure my parents would love to hear this story from someone else that was there for the entire time also."

"Duhuhhh," Yurri said while nervously tugging his collar, not meeting her eyes. "I'm not sure I can go with you Jan. I got my job with Mr. Withers, my parents would flip out if my boss tells them that I suddenly disappeared off the face of the planet, and besides that I think it would be a very embarrassing situation for me to see your parents at all. I mean you have been on the run from them for a while now and I don't think it would be healthy for me to meet them at all." He shrugged helplessly.

Yurri was being stubborn for some reason. If Janice couldn't get him to come along with her home, her parents would marry her off as soon as her ship docked! She, at least, needed to bring a prospective husband home with her to curb her mother's anxiety about her getting married. She was over twenty right now and it would make her mother go into fits the longer it took her to find a man! Janice had never even thought about marriage until she was twenty. Her older sister was in line for the throne so even though she had received the same lessons growing up as her sister did, she never really took her responsibility as a princess all that seriously. She was having too much fun running around with her friends. And then her mother went and chose a husband for her! She, of all people, should know about forced marriage arrangements. Janice remembered that her mother was going to go through an arranged marriage herself before she met her daddy. One of the few reasons she upset Janice's grandparents so much. Although… whether or not her older sister would take up the political mantle of their mother was a very tender subject in their family.

"Yurri, when have you ever gotten into an embarrassing situation with me?" she laughed, trying to curb his decision patting his shoulder playfully.

"Yesterday at that costume store," he said flatly with his arms crossed.

Oh, that was right. Though it had been very flattering that all those men were stunned by her body, but she could never modestly say that she was *that* beautiful. "I don't think I caused *that* much of a fuss."

"You flattened a couple dozen men. I think that counts as making a fuss."

Janice blushed a tad at that comment and thought it was a bit exaggerated. That occurrence wasn't really entirely her fault though! She had been a brain-dead pink head when it happened! She couldn't be held accountable for things she did as an idiot when with those stupid invoking hair colors! She needed to turn this conversation around. She had to convince him to come with her. "Yurri," she said sounding a little desperate. How could she turn this around? "Yurri… do you really think that those men that are after me would truly leave you or me alone after we leave and separate?"

He gave her this weird look his face turning a little colored. Was he trying to suppress a sigh? "Jan I…" His face was going a little purple by now. Maybe he was trying to suppress a sigh.

The princess decided to play another card. One that she thought would be easier for him to accept. "All right, Yurri," she said putting her hands out in front of her with her palms facing towards him. "Do what you want. I'm sure I'll be all right going all by myself all the way back to my spaceship which is on the other side of this city all alone. It'll only take the rest of today to get there by myself. I'm sure all those men who are after me won't find me as I travel all those long and abandoned city streets all by myself all alone." He grimaced. It was working so she hid her smirk by looking away from him turning her body.

The young man inhaled deeply then let out a long breath. "Okay you've convinced me, but only to the spaceport. You have a lot to answer for!" He glared at her sternly that was pleasant in a way to Janice. He really did care about her. "And one of those answers that I have yet to receive is how I got up on that bed last night," he said pointing to the bed.

It looked like he wanted to change the subject. This was good. Janice thought she had enough time with her boyfriend to convince him to come with her all the way to her home planet. Maybe she could say that those men saw Yurri too in that encounter and wouldn't leave him alone either. And after all they couldn't rely on the local police. They were too busy with immediate crimes and couldn't look into helping some random folk with no evidence backing up their claim. Considering the ruckus at that farming mansion with them stealing one of their vehicles it would be much healthier to fix this on their own. Along with keeping Sixy safely secret.

"Something you should know about me is that with what comes with personality shifts with different hair colors also comes variable talents and abilities that are in tune with those specific hair types." He gave her one of those oh so familiar perplexed looks. She laughed, honestly delighted in his befuddlement. "Okay, let me be more specific about that. While a brunet I'm more leveled minded and can think things through more statistically. With my hair black I am able to draw information from my memory a lot more easily. As a red head I can access all the self-defense classes I went through growing up along with the reflexes that come along with them. And I'm pretty sure you know how I am as a blonde otherwise you weren't paying that much attention to me for all those months," she finished while playfully bending down a little looking up at his face. "So considering all that self-defense training I've had you were easy enough to get standing up and to drag over to the bed. You were way conked out of it last night!"

"You're really that strong?" he asked in disbelief.

"Yup, you've never seen me do anything impressive because, as a blond, I can't access any of the reflexes I have or my self-defense training easily. Though right now with purple hair I think I can show you a demonstration," she said to him bending down a little bit again playfully looking into his eyes.

"I'm not even going to try to hit you," he told her with a chivalrous tone in his voice with his arms crossed. "I could never hit a woman." This was one of the reasons she thought Yurri was too decent at times. It was a cute type of behavior, but it could be wearing at times.

"You don't have to try to hit me or anything. Just come and try to grab me. Have fun with it! I mean, wouldn't you like another hug from me?" she asked teasingly taking a couple steps away from him while shifting her hips a little in an alluring manner playfully. She took Sixy off her neck and put him on the bed table and told him to stay there. "If you're able to grab me you get the reward of ten minutes of *requited* snuggling!"

Yurri blushed looking away from her and raking his fingers through his hair again. "You are so stressful to be around," he said still not looking at her. "Ok I'll just grab you. Then we gotta head out. Those guys might be right on our heels."

He started at her suddenly wanting to get this demonstration done and over with quickly. As he reached both of his arms at her, she grabbed one, shifted her weight just right, and threw him over her shoulder onto the bed. She didn't want to hurt him after all. He made a funny doofing grunt and bounced off it to the other side to the floor.

"Oh! Are you ok Yurri?" she asked with her hands to mouth again. "I didn't mean to toss you that hard!"

"No I guess I deserved that…" She came around the bed and saw that he was lying face down on the floor.

"Did I hurt you Yurri?" she asked worriedly. She honestly didn't mean to harm him at all. Just demonstrate one of her talents.

"You didn't hurt anything except my pride," he said still face down on the floor. "Which, by the way, I don't think I have much of anymore," he said to the carpet.

Janice came to him and helped him to stand up again. Once he was up and ready, she started gathering their things, which wasn't much, and packed them away in a complimentary tote bag and her purse. Yurri took a complimentary mint from the bed stand and popped it in his mouth. "Hey Jan, do you have any idea why those guys are after us?" he asked his girlfriend.

"I'm not really sure myself but I do have some assumptions."

"Such as?" Yurri asked opening the door for Janice.

"This is only a guess but one of the reasons those men are after me could be that they were sent from Draxus Lenox. You should know about him seeing that you used his name to distract Ron yesterday. He comes from my home planet and he is bad news. He hates my parents vehemently," she said as they walked down the hallways of the inn.

"Wait what? Draxus is an actual person with a bounty on his head? I thought I made up that name." He scratched his head as they made their way to the robotics quarter of this inn to find UP5.

"You must have heard me say his name once or something. I always read the news from my home planet throughout the day from my reading tablet. And his name is in the news often enough." She had a habit of reading aloud while a blond. It helped her concentrate on what she was doing and reading.

They reached the place where people's personal robots stayed. You didn't see a place like this very often. People of this planet treated their robots and droids with respect. They were integral when it came to mining the gas giant of Drylon for resources. On the cultures of quite a few planets droids were viewed as no more than thinking possessions and treated no better. Of course you would never hear a droid complain. They were programmed to do what they do and usually no more. No free will was programmed into them. It's that people here on this planet had a general culture of treating the machines they work with more respectfully. Anybody would if your life and livelihood depended on how well the things worked after all. Many underdeveloped planets never showed or even had the culture to show such creations much respect.

"UP5, you around here somewhere in the droids' place?" Yurri asked using his com to get a hold of the droid. Many droids don't come installed with communication devices on them, but UP5 was one of them that did apparently.

Janice heard from Yurri's com the beeps and bops UP5 usually spoke in reply to his question. Naturally Décore translated into Janice's eardrums for her. [I'm here in the facility but they had to pack me into the back. And sir I had to register myself as your droid or they wouldn't let me stay here. Could you please not tell my master about that? It's merely embarrassing. I'm his droid after all and I take pride in that.]

Janice was about to tell Yurri what UP5 had said but he was already replying to the dutiful and loyal droid by the time Décore had put the full translation through skull vibrations. "Ok we'll get you back to Tom soon. Not clear exactly what he uses you for, but you are his property. We'll get over to you soon." Maybe… he made a guess at what UP5 said.

They came around a corner and saw UP5 packed up in the back. There were many different types of droids in this place. Etiquette humanoid service droids were one of the most prevalent here, the humanoid types of droids mainly used in interspecies relationships and as just general servants too. It seemed that hotels like this were mainly for travelers that were making business deals or picking up some special resources only found on Drylon itself. These people brought business, and business brought jobs to the planet/moon and jobs meant money and money meant prosperity here. No wonder this world was flourishing. There were some cosmomaton and various other types of droids that Janice didn't really have any idea what their purposes were for around too.

They found their way quickly enough to UP5. The alcove UP5 was in was wedged in between two larger alcoves that had much bigger droids in them. They almost looked like transportation vessels. [Ah there you are,] the droid beeped unplugging itself from a wall plug. [What is our destination today?] It hovered over to them.

Janice opened her mouth to respond to the droid but Yurri beat her to it again. "I'm taking Janice to where she has her ship on the other side of this city and then I'll figure out what I'm going to do afterwards. I think you should just head on back to your boss, Tom," Yurri said waving a hand stressfully. "There are a crap load of people after us right now and besides that the experiment was botched yesterday. You don't need to stay with us." Janice stood behind Yurri as he talked with a very quizzical and befuddled look on her face. Was he actually holding a conversation with UP5? Or did what he planned to say to this droid before coincidentally sound like a conversation?

UP5 fussed with some of its compartments looking for all the worlds like a disheveled robot. Janice wondered how it did that. [Will you need the vessel I had obtained for you earlier then?] it asked still looking embarrassed somehow.

"Yes, we'll need that hover car to get over to the other side of the city," her boyfriend said. He really was holding a conversation with UP5!

[Then I'll need to accompany you. I rented that vehicle from a retailer near there. I'll need to make sure to return it properly. I had used my master's bank account number to purchase that rent and I don't want him to find out about it. He always has me and my counterparts doing his shopping for him he is so engrossed on his projects.] UP5 waved its tentacles helplessly.

"Ok you can come with us until I drop off Janice at the space port then I'll need to get over to a certain place a ways away where I left my craft and there you can take your craft back and return it." Yurri rubbed his temples stressfully.

This was too befuddling for the princess to take in completely. How did her boyfriend understand UP5? She had to use Décore to understand it and without her hair decoration she was pretty sure she wouldn't be able to understand anything at all. Yurri turned away and started to go to the exit. "Hey! Hold it right there, mister!" Janice exclaimed grabbing his arm. "Did you actually hold a conversation with UP5 or are you just messing with me?"

[You know, I've been wondering about that myself.]

She looked to UP5 a bit stunned. UP5 hadn't even realized that it was holding a conversation with Yurri too? She turned toward her boyfriend not looking amused and folded her arms underneath her chest. "Well?" she asked looking a bit impatient.

He breathed in deeply and let out a long-exaggerated sigh. That was starting to get a little annoying now. "Jan," he said putting a hand on his temples, "I honestly don't know how I can kinda understand UP5. It all sounds like beeps and bops to me. But somehow, I get the gist of what it wants to communicate to me. A lot of weird things have been going on in my life lately and I'm just trying to go with it struggling to keep my rationality at the same time too. You're a princess, a man is trying to take my life because he thinks I'm your Jai boyfriend and then there's Tom and what he made us go through…" He shrugged frowning. "I'll go along with all of this clinging to my sanity for all that its worth."

"You know," Janice said to him while coming up closer feeling sorry for him. It wasn't his fault that all these crazy things were happening to him after all. "I think I heard that some Jai or all of them, I don't know, can speak to animals." She started rubbing his shoulders a little as soon as she got near him. Gosh he was tight. "Maybe you have Jai capabilities and don't know it. I heard that the talents between Jai vary greatly so maybe you're able to communicate with droids or machines or something like that. When did you start noticing you could understand UP5? I remember that you couldn't understand UP5 at all just before we got up to that alien encampment place that we ran from. Did something in particular happen to you that is maybe Archai related while we were apart?" It really helped that her hair was purple now. Reasoning and sifting through her memories and coming to decent conclusions was immensely easier now.

Yurri patted her hands thanking her for the rub and continued through the door away from the droid part of the hotel. He looked like he was muddling over his memories for an answer to her question. They were now making their way back to the front desk.

As soon as they arrived there Janice paid for their room and all the meals they had and a good tip too. Coupled with the money she saved in a secret bank account she had purchased some small businesses covertly back at home too so she always contained herself and lived as modestly as she could during her trips from home. This way she could live her life comfortably without ever notifying her parents of her whereabouts. A trick that was taught to her by her eldest sister Laura. Janice even paid for UP5's oil bath it had while here. She didn't say anything about it though. She thought UP5 deserved the pampering after all the help it's been in with all this madness. She didn't know how it did it but UP5 somehow managed to look embarrassed and ashamed when it saw the bill as she paid it. Maybe she should offer Mr. Tom to buy UP5 from him too. It was such a nice dear droid. And she thought Yurri was coming to like it too. Though she didn't think Tom or UP5 would want to be separated. Quite a few relations between owners and droids got rather personal. Droids practically become family members. Janice could understand that very well. Décore was like a sister to Janice she's known her little droid for so long, almost literally her whole life, and could never even think of parting from her.

    Yurri rubbed his temples again as they arrived in the parking lot outside. He looked like he had been searching through his memories pretty hard trying to come up with an answer for Janice. "I can remember that Jai guy, after he saved me from those hideous alien females, do something that made me shiver. He told me to stand by a tree and looked into my eyes. Said he was checking my health or something like that. It felt like a wave of something pass over me." He shook his head shivering.

    Janice smiled as she pointed to their hover car finding it in the maze of other vehicles. She had heard many tales about the new Jai and their exploits. She was very interested in hearing about them and had a habit of checking on the news about them all the time. Quite a few people, who could remember the old Jai order, said that the new Jai out there could do some surprising things and that they were even stronger than the old Jai order completely. She believed she had heard that Jai of the healing profession could scan a person's vitals to check their overall health using the Archai. She told this to Yurri as he politely opened a door for her. He was so polite and must have been raised very well. The blond in her, her various personalities always reflected themselves minutely even while not currently that hair color, thought she just might have to take him up on that proposal.

"Maybe his touching your mind with the Archai triggered something in your brain and unlocked hidden unconscious talents that you have with the Archai," she said while buckling herself in.

Yurri groaned as he buckled himself into the driver's seat. "Aaagh, I don't want to be a Jai. They have to be respectable all the time and what's worse is they have to deal with politicians," he said turning on the vehicle. "All politicians do is feed the people lies to get votes and never go through with their promises. Lobbying themselves into certain evil organizations just to get more money and power," he said pulling out their vehicle after UP5 had latched itself onto the back seat.

Janice knew, from personal experience, about the type of politicians he was talking about. But she felt he was uniformed about how it really worked in the political spectrum of things. Her mother and father had vastly changed how things worked on her home planet. Her mother, with the help of her father, had written new laws that allowed the people of their world substantially more freedom than the people have ever enjoyed before. Daddy had introduced the idea of more freedom to the people would bring more prosperity to them all! And it worked too! And the way that she and her siblings had been raised she suspected that queenship of their planet would become an elected office with decent term limits to avoid corruption. She certainly would never like to deal with all the crap her parents dealt with on a daily basis!

The two started talking politics and various historical occurrences as Yurri drove them to their destination. It was going to take all day to get there. They were in the city now and traffic was its usual murderous self. In town vehicles were only hover crafts. Hover technology was immensely cheaper with easier upkeep than flight. A person could only adjust their elevation by a couple yards with any type of hover car and since this was a fairly new colony and hover transportation only seemed practical more so than anything else. This planet didn't have that high of a population yet, so things were more grounded here right now.

Currently, they got off the internal more crowded roads and were on a high-speed highway where only a few various hover cars were traveling with them, there were four various types of hover cars in front of them. The one in the front was a massive long bedded white transportation vehicle with a huge probably loaded trailer it was hauling. There was a red hover car, pretty long by looks of it, trailing behind that truck. Since they were in a three-lane road there was a hover vehicle of a twin design to the one behind the truck trailing behind the one behind the truck on the left lane this one red too. The last blue smaller hover car that was in front of them was tailing the others a little way back from all the rest. Yurri kept a safe distance behind them thinking that they long lost the men that were after them not in too much of a hurry.

Out of nowhere that big truck's hover capacitors decided to turn off. It slid on the ground making a spectacular display of sparks coming out from underneath it. The back of it swerved to the right blocking most of the road. The hover car behind it hit it head on making its tail end veer in front of its twin getting it to crash too. This forced the cars into a weird Z formation which made the last trailing blue hover car to hit the last red one in front of it making it fly over the one it hit and some of the rest end over end and over the trailer.

AN ORBITING DILEMMA

    Yurri quickly put on the brakes forcing the hover car to veer off to the left a little. He quickly parked their vehicle and got out to see if he could offer any help. Janice remembered him telling her that he had received some basic first aid training while he had served sometime in the army the little that she knew about him.

    Janice watched worriedly from the car not knowing what to do or how to help. She did the only thing she could think of. She whipped out her communicator and dialed an emergency number. But as she dialed blue wide stunning rays hit her. When she fell back in her seat with her purse strap over her neck her eyesight faded and blurred as she dropped her phone. As she fell into unconsciousness, she thought she saw some men come up to their vehicle and viciously stab UP5 with a rod that made fierce blue electric bolts shoot out from the droid. All was blackness.

    Yurri woke up in the back of the hover vehicle all dazed. He sat himself up trying to orient himself. The last thing he remembered was a bad car wreck happening in front of them. He had gotten out seeing if he could help any. Then after only a couple steps from their vehicle he could remember a searing electric pain pulsating from his neck down. What happened?

    He turned his head to see who was driving and his neck creaked painfully. He grabbed at it and felt some burnt skin. He jerked his hand away in surprise then slowly placed a hand on the burn testing and feeling out the damage.

    He heard some beeping noises coming from the front seat. Was that UP5 up there? He turned to look, and it was UP5 in one of the front seats with someone else driving this hover car. "Whoa there, buddy. You should lay there still. It will take about half an hour for your system to reconfigure itself after receiving that shock from that tazer," the driver said.

Yurri shook his head. His vision was still a little blurry from waking up. He looked around for Janice and didn't see her. "Where's Janice?"

"The princess was taken by those men from Draxus Lenox. It's my fault they got her. I should have been watching you two more closely."

Wait, who was he talking to? Yurri's neck ached with pain a little as he looked to the driver of this vehicle. "Rialin? Rialin Epoch? Jai master Rialin Epoch?" he asked a couple times confused with his situation. He thought this guy was out looking for that lost princess of planet Tyy. Oh wait, the same princess who happened to be Janice. After all the confusion lately he had totally forgotten about this guy.

"The one and the same, your head will clear in about half an hour," the Jai told him again thinking that Yurri was still dazed. "Since I don't work well with civilians, I'll drop you off at a safe place if I see one and then I'll continue my search for the princess. I called orbital security, so no ship gets off this planet without an inspection first. They won't get away from me."

Yurri sat himself up back in the seat at first calmed down a little by what Rialin told him. Then he thought about the situation more thoroughly and came to the conclusion that the Jai was lying to him. There was no orbital security that could monitor the countless ships that came and went from a high marketing planet like this one. The Jai didn't want the involvement of useless civilians in a crisis like this. Yurri looked around and saw that this was the same hover car he had been in before the attack.

"Come on man. I want and need to help. Even if they can't get off planet right now you would still need to search the whole city or planet. I promise to not get in your way. I think you could always use another set of eyes. Also I think we should call the local police force to help us," Yurri pleaded and reasoned with the Jai.

"Calling for help isn't an option," the Jai said grimly. "Draxus is well known to 'clean up' quickly any hostage situation he's in if he gets overwhelmed. He's already killed eight hostages when a good force came after him when they thought they had Draxus cornered. I'm sure he has someone monitoring the police lines right now just for that. Also he knows that we know he's on the planet." The Jai sighed. "In any case, if you want to help, do you have any way to track her? That would be helpful. If not, I'm going to drop you off. I don't need you to risk your life also. The people I'm after are the type to shoot first and ask questions later," the Jai said. So Janice was right. Her home planet crime lord was after her.

UP5 gave out various beeps telling Yurri that it might be able to track down Janice. Yurri sat up with abrupt attention looking at UP5 ignoring the way his head swam. "UP5 you can track Janice? How?" he asked the perplexing droid. What other hidden talents did it have? UP5 gave him the impression that it could track Janice through her clothing. After some more discussions the young man found out that the mad scientist Tom always put tracking devices on all his clothing. A weird habit he picked up from his mother.

Yurri told this to Rialin excited to be part of Janice's rescue team. "Wait man," the Jai said shaking his head. "You're telling me that you can understand what that droid is saying even without a translator handy?"

The young man didn't know how to answer that without sounding crazy. "Janice says I… might be Archai sensitive because of it but I don't know. I just want to help you somehow to get Janice back," Yurri said helplessly. He didn't enjoy having this new talent of his very much, but he would use it if it helped Janice.

"Actually this might be to our benefit," the Jai said as he pulled their vehicle over to the side near a sidewalk and parked with various hover cars passing them by. The Jai got out and headed to the back where Yurri was. This road didn't look like it got much traffic. The Jai motioned to Yurri to stay seated when Yurri started to get himself out. "Just sit there calmly for me. This will only take a minute or two. Rialin reached out and touched Yurri's temples on either side of his head with both hands. The Jai stood there concentrating on something not focusing his gaze on the young man's face. All of a sudden, the Jai was lifted up into the air about a foot and was shoved away about a yard forcefully. This didn't startle the man at all. He actually smiled as he caught his footing after landing.

This may have not startled the Jai too much, but it did just that with Yurri. "What the frell was that!" Yurri knew something had happened. Rialin didn't jump back or anything like that. He actually levitated into the air and was shoved back.

"That, my friend, is how the Jai of this new order go about finding other Archai sensitive individuals," the Jai said waving his hands to calm Yurri down. "The old Jai order did something with checking somebody's bone marrow or something like that, but that knowledge has been completely wiped away with the Kaiser Kahn's purge of the old Jai order," Rialin said shaking his head. "In the High Q clan, or the nickname of the Highquasar family, a generation or so ago they discovered this new way to find Archai sensitive individuals. We just need to lightly sift through your brain touching it alerting it to an Archai user then go down to your heart. This triggers a reflexive action through the Archai. A defensive reaction we think. In the past the Jai order kept things like this extremely secret. Not even regular members of that old order knew exactly how it was done. This means you could become a Jai if you applied yourself."

This revelation threw poor Yurri for a loop. He honestly never wanted to become more than what he was. Maybe start a business with his dad or some of his old friends working with machinery but nothing like this. He was a very non-confrontational type of guy. He thought to become a medical aid or something like that for the military. "So wait, how does this help us? It takes months, even years for someone to learn and wield the Archai properly enough to become a Jai. We don't have that sort of time." Yurri shrugged helplessly still befuddled by the Jai's excitement.

"Yes we don't, but luckily for us I have a certain talent that I thought was fairly useless before this." The young man gave the Jai a mixed look looking between baffled, like he was so often these past few days, and trepidation in his face. "I can impart certain talents and abilities I have to other people." Rialin said with his face filling with consternation. "Though it only works once on any individual and usually they get a horribly painful headache for a couple days after it wears off, which usually takes about a month. The few studies on this show that artificial memories slowly deteriorate until the artificial memory pathways collapse on themselves. I haven't really explored this ability of mine all that much. My family and my job as a Jai demand too much of my time for me to do any experiments with it." Rialin shrugged looking resigned to that fact.

"So what you're saying is that you can actually make me a Jai, even temporarily, so we both can go out and rescue Janice?" Yurri honestly didn't know how he should feel about this. Maybe a little excited that he can be of more help to the Jai in rescuing Janice and get all those cool powers but still there was a part of him that was horrified by the responsibility that those powers would invoke on him to bear also. He honestly didn't want too much out of life, simply the things his parents had. A home and a family with a good job too. Not much at all.

Yurri sighed heavily once again. He needed to stop doing that. Janice grimaced at him the last time he did it around her. "Ok man let's get this over with. What do you need me to do?"

"Come on out of the car. I'll need the space to work on you. This will only take about five minutes or so. It would take longer if I gave you all of my experiences and talents but since we don't have much time, I'll just unlock certain latent abilities you have stored in your unconscious and give you some of the rudimentary skills to wield the Archai and luminblades." Yurri got out and stepped up in front of the Jai. "Alright I will need to touch your head and it will feel quite odd." Rialin put his hands on Yurri's forehead.

While this was going on the young man had to admit that it did feel extremely weird. An uncomfortable vibrating sensation pulsed into his head coming from the Jai's hands. This experience felt similar to stretching out your body painfully while rapidly cramming marshmallows down your throat at the same time too. This was an exceptionally strange experience for the young fellow.

The young man fell to his knees once the Jai let go of his head. Yurri panted and sweated as he reached for his face. His memories were all being jumbled around while the Jai was doing whatever he was doing to his head. He searched his memories and could actually remember dueling someone with a luminblade! He looked out in front of himself and saw the hover vehicle that UP5 had rented. Impulsively he reached out his right hand. The hover car started lifting high into the air. After it had risen about a dozen yards into the air UP5, who was still in that craft, started flipping out making wild beeps and bops swinging its tentacles around in a panicked manner. Yurri released his hold on the craft and it swiftly came down. Good thing it had its repulsor lifts on. It slammed to the ground with a surprisingly soft crash.

"Wow that actually worked," the Jai said getting a surprised look from Yurri. He looked at the young man and tried to explain himself. "The last couple of times I tried that out the poor guys started running in circles on the floor while shrieking gibberish." Rialin gave him a shrug embarrassed.

"You know… you could have mentioned that to me before dude." The exasperated young man said shaking his head. A thought popped up in Yurri's mind when he looked at the Jai again. How had this guy followed them from the wilderness near that rich guy's place and then found them when they got attacked by those guys a second time? It was miles from the city and how had he been there at the right time to save Yurri in the first place? Had this guy been following them? Yurri looked to the Jai and asked him these questions.

The Jai nodded saying, "Yes I have been following you two. You think I didn't get a holo image and some information of the princess I was after?" The young man shrugged, and the Jai continued his explanation. "I thought that if I let you two wander around a bit more it would attract Draxus Lenox out of hiding. From what I know about him he is the type of mobster who likes to get his hands dirty. It was my mistake in not filling you two into my plans that got her kidnapped from us. I suspect that he has a hidden vessel somewhere located in this city or around it. It's probably only a small fighter with warp capabilities to use to slip by planet security. I had been following you two with a rented speeder bike. I left it behind though after I saved you from Draxus's goonies."

Yurri shook his head and thought he should have probably figured most of that out himself. Lately it's been too insane for him to think clearly at all. When a weird buzzing sound came from above them the young man and Jai looked up to see a man with a jet pack on coming toward them about twenty feet in the air. He was zooming towards them. It was Ron! Yurri's jaw fell open once he recognized the man. He had completely forgotten about Janice's old crazy bounty hunter boyfriend. "Friend of yours?" the Jai asked the young man. As Yurri shook his head the bounty hunter opened fire on them as if to clarify Yurri's answer.

Yurri jumped out of the way behind the hover car while the Jai calmly ignited his deep green luminblade to deflect laser blasts and grabbed at something in the pouch he had around his waist. From it he threw out five small fist sized blue orbs that flew towards the rocketing Ron in the air. Two of those orbs slammed into Ron's chest knocking him for a loop. Ron stopped firing at them recognizing that he was in trouble. But Rialin wasn't done with him yet; the other three orbs hit Ron at various spots on his body. Two of those orbs struck his feet at the exact time as the other one shot into the man's crotch while the last two that had hit him in the chest slammed into his head on either side. Ron spun crazily out of control to the ground but before he hit the ground Rialin's flying blue orbs somehow unwound themselves into blue pieces of rope about two yards long each. The blue ropes now caught and wrapped around each of Ron's limbs with one going around his stomach.

With Ron contained in such a way the Jai lowered him to the ground with a not so comfortable plop on the ground near them. Once on the ground Rialin shifted how the blue ropes were positioned on Ron's body neatly tying him up around his ankles with his hands being tied behind his back by the odd blue ropes.

After this was done the Jai levitated the man in front of himself and Yurri and he gave the young man a questioning look asking him what now. Yurri, impressed at the ease the Jai took control of the situation, thought about what he could do now with the troublesome man. He undoubtedly still wanted very much to hurt Yurri right now for tricking him yesterday. Though now as Yurri thought about it might be a good idea to bring along another fella who knew how to use a blaster in their search and inevitable fight with Draxus's goonies.

"Hold him there for me Rialin. Let me see if I can't convince this man to join us with looking for Janice." The Jai gave Yurri a questioning look, so the young man tried to elaborate. He explained to the Jai how this mess all started with Ron crashing his brunch date with Janice yesterday. "This man isn't too bright upstairs so I'm hoping with a little help from Jai wit dominance we can convince this guy to help us in getting Janice back."

Rialin looked at him and nodded thinking it over in his head. "I think it would be easier to control this man for long periods of time if we had something of material value to offer him. In everyone they reflexively resist Jai wit dominance. If you have something to offer him as a reward that would distract his conscious thoughts enough for long periods of time. Getting them to think it was their idea to do what we want."

Ron moaned only halfway conscious. Rialin must have dropped him to the ground harder than Yurri thought. The young man thought fast on what he could offer Ron in exchange for his help. A nasty thought popped into the young man's head. "Hey UP5, do we still have that hotel baggie filled with our stuff in there?" UP5 beeped a positive to his question. "Hand it to me please. I need to get something from it." The droid gave Yurri the baggie through an open window.

The Jai viewed this curiously while he kept an eye on Ron who was still a bit under though getting some color back to his face floating suspended in front of the professional Jai. Yurri found what he was looking for and brought it out for everyone to see. It was one of those bottles of cologne that him and Jan had received from that mad scientist, Tom, to test out with that holo disk too. "What's that for?" the Jai asked Yurri.

"It's a long story," Yurri said not wanting to get into it fully. "But this is the reason that those hideous Enohps were chasing me first time we met. It makes them crazy in love with anyone that puts this stuff on." It was one of the bottles that Tom had given him, but it wasn't the red one. He couldn't find that one anywhere in the bag. Maybe he used too much of it and/or Jan threw it away. Couldn't blame her. Oh well Yurri thought. This bottle came from Tom so the same results could be expected from it too. At least he had that mini holo-projector with the image of that spectacularly alluring alien female. The young man explained his plan to the Jai and showed him the holo.

"That is downright devious and a little bit on the dark side, but you haven't decided to fully become a Jai yet so let's see if this works." Rialin levitated Ron in front of him and gave him a good slap. "I hate dealing with bounty hunters so wake up quickly so we can get started on our business," the Jai said in an angry tone of voice to the bounty hunter putting on a show.

Ron's awakening was a startled jerk when Rialin slapped him one more time. Yurri licked his lips hoping that his plan and new-found skills would work out to convincing the bounty hunter to help them.

Yurri was now driving the hover car while following UP5's directions. It looks like those thugs were making their way toward the central part of the city. Those guys seemed to have made quite a gain on them too. With the direction they were going right now they would reach the central park soon.

The central park for this city actually had its own ecosystem totally independent of the city it was so huge surrounded by the exceptional city. This colony was very proliferous after all.

A thought popped into the young man's head while he was driving stressfully. Why didn't those guys try kidnapping Janice earlier? Why today of all days? A loose thought came in having him think this might have something to do with Dism getting so close to finding his god child. The hover car bumped slightly forcing Yurri to forget that thought and to contemplate more puzzling matters.

The young man turned Jai looked behind him to see the bounty hunter riding in the back with the Jai Rialin. He was kind of surprised at how easily Ron had come to the conclusions and thinking they wanted him to. Yurri believed that Ron didn't need to have wit dominance on him to convince him to help them after the young man had shown him the holo with the amazingly beautiful alien woman in it. Well Rialin did tell him that the simpler the intended target's mind was the easier it was to put them under their control.

Yurri sighed heavily thinking what his life had come to. He grimaced thinking how Janice doesn't like him doing that. She being a princess and all she would need a boyfriend who looked worthy of her. He grimaced again thinking about how he felt about his girlfriend suddenly becoming a princess. Maybe he should tell her it would never work out between them after they saved her. After all she had been using him as nothing more than to help aid her disguise. He was pretty sure she would be going back to her parents after all of this. If they were able to save her that was. Ach, who was he kidding? Their relationship was over the instant he found out she was a princess. And what really did he know about her? Since the time he first met her she hadn't really told him anything about herself. From the way she acted around him for the months he knew her she acted only like a trophy girlfriend, stupid, only wanting to be seen with him, and quite blond. And now, to his most dire surprise, he had found out she was vastly more than he ever thought she was. A brilliant tactical minded beauty who could defend herself quite well, and who could change her talents and abilities in the blink of an eye, how was he supposed to be worthy of that? Of course he could put in the effort to become a full Jai, but having these powers made him feel unconscionably uncomfortable. After all his father had taught him that power corrupts. Too many political things would be thrust into his life also if he pursued a relationship with Janice, and he just can't stand politicians.

He sighed again drawing it out at extra length to solidify his decision to break up with Janice after they saved her. He followed UP5's directions almost unconsciously now he was so troubled by inner demons.

To distract him from other uncomfortable thoughts Yurri thought to start a conversation with Ron, finding more out about this nasty yet stupid bounty hunter. "Hey Ron, why was it that you thought that I was a Jai before?" Ron undoubtedly believed that he was a true Jai anyways right now.

Ron told him that Janice had always talked about Jai and the latest exploits she heard about them doing. She even had a poster holo of Jim Highquasar in the apartment where she used to live. This was new to Yurri. He hadn't a clue where Janice had been staying since she got here. She had never invited him over to where she was living on this planet. And apparently Ron knew her originally as a brunette. They had dated for one-month tops before she broke up with him. Her changing her hair color to blond was what really threw him off. Apparently, Ron had some amazing connections to information resources. He was vague on telling exactly how that was but Yurri got the impression that his information mainly came from some family ties. The way this fellow actually found them here in the city was purely by accident.

He had been randomly wandering around the city with his jet pack then all of a sudden stumbled on to them. How in the worlds did this guy ever become a halfway productive bounty hunter? And why is he even still alive with a profession like that? The information Yurri was able to glean off Ron didn't come easily. He kept on staring at the holo they gave him drooling slightly. Maybe that was because of the recent head trauma Yurri thought. He hoped so anyways or otherwise it was a very impressive thing for Janice to have stood up with him for a complete month.

Yurri had removed the itchy neck attachment that came along with his alien costume by this time. They had already found them so what does it matter? His skin was still purple, and his hair was still green from the dye he used. You needed to use special shampoo that came with the buy of this costume to fully get it out. He randomly thought what all this costume stuff was made out of to distract his mind from thinking about how he would have to break up with Janice after all this.

Soon they were pulling into the enormous central park area. It was a literal forest that wasn't kept up for looks. There were parks made on the outside of the city just for that. Yurri felt a little guilty at not knowing why people on this planet had left such an area alone after being here for so long. He didn't have good skills in trying to find things out.

Animals could usually be seen and heard if you searched hard enough for them. But that's not what they were here for now. The young man concentrated on finding his way through the trees.

UP5 beeped to Yurri that they were getting close. "How close UP5?" he asked the helpful droid. It beeped at him again saying that it could sense the signal a ways into the huge central park. The young man drove them into the park and told UP5 when they got within a mile of these guys to tell him. They only got about a mile or two into the park before they started having vehicle troubles.

"What's the problem?" the Jai asked getting out with Yurri to check on some wiring on the vehicle. They opened the hood and it looked like it was working perfectly so Yurri didn't know and he told the Jai that. UP5 got out and stated to Yurri, through some beeps and bops that the reason why this city has such a spectacularly large center park was because of the special types of minerals it had underneath the surface of it here. These minerals were common enough in quite a few asteroid fields and on other planets in this solar system so no one thought to go about removing them for profit. These specific types of minerals interfered with hover technology disabling it completely. This was why this city had such an enormous central park. As the city grew throughout the years it grew around this area leaving it alone completely. The minerals didn't have much good use for them anyways, they were mainly an annoyance to anybody in general. And it would be horrifically expensive to remove the vast amount that's deep underground anyways.

Yurri told what the droid had told him to the Jai but looked to the droid again still a little confused. "So wait, if this place messes up hover technology why aren't you grounded as well?" the young man asked the droid who was obviously not having any problems at all with hovering. UP5 let out some weird motions that somehow displayed it being embarrassed again yet still with a touch of pride in it. Yurri wondered how it did that but reasoned it must be because of his weird talent with the Archai in understanding droid speak. It relayed to him that it's master, crazy old Tom, had figured out how to make repulsor lift technology that worked even here.

Yurri was about to ask the droid why Tom didn't sell this technology to the general public when Rialin interrupted him. "I'm not sure how relevant it is that we know how this droid is able to hover here but we're on a mission to save the princess of planet Tyy right now. UP5 exactly how far away are we from them right now?" the Jai asked the droid in a stern but impatient tone.

Yurri raked his hand through his green hair stressfully embarrassed that he went off on that tangent there. UP5 communicated to him that they were a bit away from them still, but they could catch them soon even if they walked. They haven't moved for quite some time now so UP5 was confident that they had stopped somewhere for some reason. As Yurri translated for the Jai a plot of action came in the young man's head as they started making their way through the forest.

Yurri started asking questions about the Jai's abilities and found out that the reason why the Jai had those blue orb ropes with him was because if a Jai trained themselves to do a certain thing with the Archai it would of course become easier and reflexive. While doing anything with the Archai it would drastically dull your defensive skills. So Rialin had thought to have useful items to carry with him everywhere and so these special blue spheres were the outcome of that. His wife made them herself and Rialin had trained for months and years on end to develop this special talent of his. The more personal an item was to you the more it became a part of your Archai senses too. His talent was that he could move these orbs around independent of each other, very useful in chaotic situations and keep moderate defensive skills too. Yurri then asked the droid what it knew about the general layout of this place and a decent plan of attack started forming in Yurri's head as they made their way which he shared with the Jai, Ron, and UP5.

The princess woke up very disoriented and confused with her situation. What was happening? She found herself bound and tied around her wrists in front of her along with her ankles on the ground with a quite a few men around her too all working on something that looked like it was supposed to be a small fighter space craft with her face on pokey grassy ground. Where was Yurri? What happened to him? A man noticed that she had woken up and came over to her from where others were working on putting that ship together with a lewd look on his face. Janice couldn't bring out any words she was so afraid of this man. The stocky black haired though graying man couldn't be anyone else. This was Draxus Lenox!

"Aww, Princess Janiece Agra," this man said while giving her a mock bow, "so good of you to join us." This man was wearing some serious hardware on his body. Janice was unable to tell where the machinery on his body started and where his actual clothing ended. From what she could remember about him was that he had a fetish for biomechanical weapons and armor.

"Don't you worry now little princess," he said coming over to her grinning wickedly. "After all I've went through to get your sorry hide, I won't let anything happen to you until I'm done with you." He bent down and grabbed her by the hair painfully pulling her up to face him. Janice cried out in pain at first but stopped when the evil man slapped her face. "There will be none of that now my sweet little princess. You don't know the pains I went to find your pampered hide. While you were away from home your daddy finally found a way to put me out of operation." The big man clenched his free hand with pure and only slightly controlled fury on his face. "This is where you come in," he said with a very libidinous look on his face. "Now please don't hold anything back," he chuckled. "I'm counting on you to scream for me after we get you off this rock. I will send your screams to your daddy and mommy just to accentuate the point of my demands. Along with a lock of your hair just to prove we have you. My men and I will be having lots of fun with you to encourage a good show from you for your parents."

The princess was crying openly now trying to curl herself up into a fetal position while in the air. Why wasn't she able to get a hold of herself? As a small child and a teenager she had survived several hostage situations just like this and had remained calm like she had been trained to do. A lock of her hair fell on her face and she saw that it was blond! That explained her reaction to this situation but why was her hair blond?

The evil man saw her reaction and rightly guessed what was on her mind. "You have no idea what pains I took to make sure this operation went smoothly as possible." He threw her to the ground punching all the breath away from Janice. "Of course I already know of your mutation with your hair and how it affects your talents. When we tracked you here on this planet it didn't take long to discern what you're like with that hair color. You don't know how much you simplified matters when my informants found out what you were like as a blond. I want you to have a full understanding of what we're doing to you with no veil of ignorance." He looked down at her again giving her that vulgar look again making her feel filthy. "All we had to do was to hack your hair droid and freeze it on one setting. It's obviously working because I know you. You have escaped far worse situations than this before."

The gang leader was right. Janice was so scared right now she couldn't get herself to stop sobbing uncontrollably or to unfreeze herself from the fetal position. What pained her most was the thought of that man sending her screams to her parents. The pain it would cause them dug deep into Janice's mindset.

"Oh and to top this little excursion off," Draxus said in an offhanded manner. "I'm planning to destroy one of

Dism Quantum's farming plantations and possibly kill him too in the meantime. With a droid I had 'acquired' named X2-O0 from one of Dism's friendlier business competitors." The gangster waved a hand to the left and walked back where they were working on that machine.

Uncle Dism was here? Her parents probably asked him to search for her when she disappeared. She had to escape to warn him! Janice struggled to turn herself to see what Draxus had waved at. It was an enormous monster of a vicious looking battle droid or battle transportation vehicle. It was black gray and of the size of a multi –legged tank walker as was used in the war with the old Kaiser Kahn. The evil old villain dictator had used many variations of those to track down the rebel alliance. This one was vaguely humanoid though. The thick machine looked bipedal with reversed knee joints. It was headless with one huge red orb where the neck should be that was possibly the eye for this machine. For some reason it had many compartments across its entire body. It had four arms coming out of its torso with what looked like an assortment of switch out blades and tools used for who knew what. With this thing it was very possible all those tools had a violent purpose behind them.

She heard some growling coming behind her, she rolled over to see what it was, she was still terrified, but her training had been extensive to the point where it was reflexive to search out the area she was in determining her resources. All she wanted to do right now was stay in the fetal position and sob into her chest. She saw a man with eight enormous fearsome looking pale-yellow cat-like collared beasts with long snouts that came up to his higher midsection at his side talking to another man. "Don't you think it a little excessive to bring these biological weapons with us just to kidnap a princess like her?"

His friend shook his head and groaned himself. "I don't see why myself, but you know the boss. He has to plan for every contingency. And I've heard that this particular princess is quite a nasty hostage to have. I heard that one time this princess took down a whole gang of alien mercenaries by herself in a city on planet Tyy. She took them out with a weird type of weapon. Haven't heard what that was though. Guess no one survived to tell others about it."

Janice remembered that but in a hazy kind of way. It must be because of her hair being blond for so long. She had a very queasy stomach when it comes to violence as a blond. All the violent things she's lived through were tucked nicely away in her unconscious until she had the stomach again to sift through those memories. Much like how she can't access any of her self-defense training while blond. Survival instincts yes but defense no. She looked around a little and found out they were in a large clearing too with a forest of trees not too far away. Tears were still streaming down her face.

The man continued to explain to his friend just why they were being so careful around her. He also explained that since Tyy was such a productive trading post many merchants wanted to make Tyy a part of their trading empire so many underhanded merchants wanted to capitalize on their prosperity, ever since the current queen had married a commoner their revenues had exploded. There have been many attempts to bring the current ruling class of that planet to heel under various gangster types it was so small and unworthy of big note. The king there had prepared for that though with him knowing the basic dastardly tricks of many underhanded merchants. Janice's father and mother had her and all her siblings go through many self-defense and strategist classes while they were growing up.

Janice was proud of her parents' foresight on how they raised her and her siblings but right now all that training had been nullified. Tears continued streaming down her cheeks and she figured she must have a puffy red face by now, but the flow of those tears had lessened considerably. She still searched for things to help her out. In the back of her mind she wondered why in the worlds they were building a starcraft here? Why not simply take her to an already constructed ship? Maybe it had to do with how this planet keeps track of interplanetary traffic. She could remember that every new ship to dock in a spaceport on this planet had to be registered and documented for later use. She didn't believe the government here did much with that information. It was probably more for marketing research. They didn't bug people here too much about it. Though whatever it was done for it apparently had spooked Draxus and his goonies enough to take serious precautions. But why start building a space craft here and now since they've obviously been here for a while watching her? Why didn't they already have it built? Maybe Draxus only recently figured out how to get her off planet without too much notice. Or maybe something unexpectedly happened forcing him to move up his timetable.

It looked like that focusing on finding what resources she had had been working to calm her nerves. Her tears were drying up while she explored her area by viewing it. There were quite a few men working on that ship of theirs. She started searching for her purse wondering where it had gotten to. She found it not a few yards away from her. They must have thought it inconsequential enough they must have let her carry it on her unconscious body. She remembered that she had Sixy packed away in there. She smiled to herself thinking what would happen to these men if she was able to get her pet out of there. At first, she only hesitated at the thought of letting Sixy out of her purse because she worried that those evil men might somehow kill her little Sixy once he was out. Right now, she couldn't worry about that. She had faith in Sixy.

She started crawling tentatively over to her purse to see if she could get it open for help from Sixy. Janice arrived and got herself into a sitting position by it. She reached over to grab her purse. "Hey!" one of Draxus's goonies yelled at her with a blaster pointed at her too. "What are you doing?" he asked still with his blaster trained on her. "If the boss catches that I let you crawl around he'll have my hide!" She grabbed at her purse putting it to her chest thinking furiously of an excuse.

"I…" she said licking her lips. She really was a terrible liar as a blond. "I wanted to get out my chap stick," she said weakly. But before the man could respond to her the ship, they were working fiercely on, unexpectedly exploded pushing Janice back. The explosion startled the man so much his blaster went off. Janice had reflexively put her purse between her and the man with the gun before the ship exploded so the purse intercepted the shot and bounced the blaster bolt safely away.

Out of nowhere these strange blue spheres zoomed in out of nowhere to knock out various men around the area. "It's a Jai!" she heard a call come out from the madness. The men that Draxus had set to form a perimeter around them were scattering everywhere and falling down knocked out by hurtling blue orbs. Blaster bolts joined the blue orbs in taking men down too by this time.

Janice looked out from behind her purse to that man who had been pointing his blaster at her earlier who was now on the ground with quite a huge bump on his forehead. And there was Yurri! "Hi Jan," he said picking her up in his strong arms. After cradling her securely in his well-toned arms he started running for a much denser part of the forest. The whole area was in chaos with those blue orbs flying around and taking many men down. Blasters were going off all around the area too. Obviously, the gangsters didn't know where the attack was coming from and were panicking. One of Draxus's henchmen saw them and positioned himself in their way yelling at Yurri to stop. Her boyfriend flung his head to the side and that man soared into the air away from them about twenty feet. He kept running with her in his arms. Janice gasped at seeing Yurri do this. Yurri actually was a Jai! He lied to her! With the chaos in this area now Yurri only had to use his Archai powers two more times to fling men out of their way. The chaos in the area was so wide-ranging they were able to escape completely into the dense forest.

    Yurri ran on carrying her effortlessly for miles, it seemed, as he ran. With her safety assured Janice broke down. While her boyfriend ran on, she sobbed onto his shoulder as she shared with him what they were planning to do with her through fits and starts of crying. He didn't talk as he ran. The young man focused on running and keeping his footing in the rooty forest. Her purse was flopping at her side still clasped tightly by her tied hands. After a long while of crying into his shoulder she began idly thinking about how a properly made tux would look on him. A blond thought of course. She looked up into his eyes and noticed that he wasn't even sweating yet. He must be in better shape than she thought. What she didn't know was that all Jai could use a technique with the Archai to wash away fatigue. Not a technique to be used for long periods of time though. There were side effects to this of course. Such as if they did this for too long their body would just give up on them or a person could run until they died on the spot. This was why you don't see Jai do this too often. You could only do so much with the Archai just like everything. It wasn't a limitless power. It drew on a person's reserves.

    After they reached a distance that Yurri was comfortable with he stopped, breathing hard. They had run zigzagging through the forest to make it hard to follow them. He gently put Janice on the ground and started searching through the multiple pockets his clothing had that Janice had picked out for him. He found what he had been looking for and brought out a decent sized switch blade. Where did he get that? It must have been one of the things she threw out of his old clothing pockets when she had sneaked into that hotel bathroom to gather up his dirty clothes. She had done that quickly not wanting to get into uncomfortable situations in a bathroom while Yurri was taking a shower. She had set up everything she found in his pockets on the bathroom counter top. The blond in her found his preparedness impressive and very attractive at this moment though that shouldn't count for much because, as a blond, she was generally easily impressed.

"Yurri," she said rubbing her wrists after standing up. "How did you find me? How did you save me? I didn't know my purse could do that! Where's UP5? You *lied* to me!!!" she yelled stamping her foot slapping his face. "You actually are a Jai! You've been lying to me for months! Why? Well? What do you have to say for yourself?" She said all that in rapid succession. Her mind had been whirling with questions after she calmed down while in his arms, but she kept them to herself once she noticed the very grim look Yurri had on his face while running with her. "Well?" she asked again after only a moment pause then opened her purse to see how Sixy was.

Poor Yurri only rubbed his cheek where Janice's slap had landed looking dumbfounded at her. Not the expected response from a woman whom he recently saved and was crying horribly on his shoulder not too long ago. "Duhhh," he said still rubbing his cheek obviously wondering which question to answer first. "After they knocked us out that Jai Rialin saved me and UP5 in that car and then we started tracking you by UP5's ability to track your clothing," Yurri said shrugging not looking at her.

That explained some but not everything she asked. And why was he not looking at her? He looked guilty about something. "That does not answer all my questions," she said sternly with Sixy in her arms. The pitiable little fellow had been freaking out since she let him out of her purse. He obviously had known something bad was happening to her. Her purse was too well made that even he couldn't get out of it if he wanted to. Janice wondered why that was. She got her purse from Daddy. He likes making things for her, her sisters, and younger brother.

"UP5 stayed out of the attack. It should still be with the Jai Rialin and Ron. Rialin and Ron attacked those guys to distract them while I got you out of there," he said with his hands up as if to defend himself. She nodded for him to continue while she was petting Sixy's head calming him down. "UP5 was able to track you because Tom puts tracking devices in all of his clothing." Janice gave him a weird look with a question on her face. He raked his hand through his green hair and explained that Tom got this weird habit from his mother of always making sure his clothing had tracking chips in them.

"That answers some of my questions but still not all," she said tapping her lips looking up at him. That clothing did look good on him. "Ohh Yurri I was so frightened!" She put Sixy down, ran up to Yurri, and embraced him in a firm hug pushing him back a bit. She obviously doesn't handle stress very well as a blond either. "You look so dashing in these clothes Yurri," she said looking up into his face after snuggling his broad muscular chest.

"Duhhhh, hey Jan," the young man said with his arms out wide. He obviously didn't know what to do with them while this girl was up around him. "I think it would be a good idea if you changed your hair color to a brunet or something that would be more helpful right now."

"I can't," she said while snuggling into his broad muscular chest again. He smelled so wonderful, a salty manly sweet scent. That must be from some deodorant he got from the hotel. Whatever it was she liked it and would look into seeing if she couldn't find more for him. Yurri asked her why not with her head still on his shoulder. "I can't because those bad men locked Décore on standby with my hair blond." She finally disengaged their embrace blushing quite a bit. She really was stressed out and scatter brained by that kidnapping.

"Really?" he asked with a dumbfounded expression on his face again. "ACH!!" he shouted throwing his hands up. "I just can't get a break today!! It's like I'm stuck in a really *badly* written comic book!!!"

Janice worriedly picked up Sixy again petting his head stressfully. "What should we do now, Yurri?" she asked him with concern etched all over her face. He'll be able to get them out of this though. She had faith in her wonderful, brave, and handsome Jai boyfriend.

"Well the plan was to first get you away while the Jai Rialin, Ron, and UP5 distracted them. Then you and I would find a place to lay low for a bit. That's why I had UP5 go with Rialin. So they could find us easily after they escaped those guys," he said while starting to pace. "Then, after we regroup, we can head back into the city and get help from the local authorities."

That sounded like a good plan to Janice. Her boyfriend always came up with good plans. So, they simply had to sit here and wait then. She looked around a bit and found a knocked down tree that looked like it would make a nice bench for now. She walked over to it and sat down. Yurri had that funny look of resignation on his face once again. She smiled at him while patting on a spot on the log inviting him to sit next to her. He sighed again making her grimace a little.

If they were going to get married, she was going to have to do something about that annoying habit of his.

He came over and sat down by her looking stressed. After she put Sixy down she started happily rubbing his shoulders which made him wince for some reason. Maybe the rub just hurt him a little. She continued doing it but only a little softer. "So Yurri why have you been keeping the fact that you're a Jai hidden from me?" she asked wondering why in the worlds he had went to such lengths as that act earlier that morning while her hair was purple. He was a pretty good actor tricking her into thinking he wasn't a Jai even before he came out and told her himself.

He sighed again, which she pinched him for, and shook his head. "I'd rather not talk about that right now Jan. How about we have a long talk about it after all of this is over? We can discuss all this stuff in a safe and sane place."

"While having dinner?" she asked loosening those knots in his broad shoulders.

He turned a little purple as he held back yet another sigh but nodded his head in a very resigned way. This was good. That could be interpreted as him meaning to come along with her home.

"You know," she said still rubbing his shoulders. He seemed to be loosening up a little by now. They didn't have much time alone until Rialin and UP5 found them, so she wanted to think of how to reward Yurri for all his heroic deeds for her. She had faith in UP5 and that very professional Jai to get to them soon enough and safely. "I know you don't want to talk about it right now, but I need to think of something to do to punish you."

"What?" he said turning to look at her obviously wondering where this had come from.

"Well for months you have been lying to me about who you really are. And something like that needs to be punished."

It didn't matter to her that she had been lying to him for months also. It was always worse for a man to lie to a woman anyways. She removed her hands from his firm shoulders and looked into his eyes slyly in a teasing manner with him so obviously lost in her mocking game. "But since you saved my life back there, I guess that means I need to reward you too," she said putting her hands on her ample hips looking seriously into his eyes pursing her full lips.

"How are you going to do that?" he asked in a way that said he wished he didn't have to find that out.

She looked behind them to make sure there were no rocks back there just soft grassy ground. After checking behind them she looked at him one more time just to check his positioning and smiled. "Oh, I don't know…" she said with him looking wary scootching a little ways away from her. She looked away from him over her shoulder. "With maybe something… like this!" The princess turned around, flung her arms around his neck in an impossibly quick manner and pulled his head down for a long and very electric toned kiss.

After releasing her victim, allowing him to fall back on soft grass, she smiled giggling into her palm. Sixy was not two feet away from her happily munching on a rodent he found and caught. Janice picked up her purse and started searching for something. She had come to a decision regarding Yurri. After looking for it in the special spot where she put it, she brought out that wonderfully beautiful ring Yurri had proposed to her with. After viewing it for a little while marveling at how beautiful it was and how well thought out a gift it was too, she put it on the proper finger. She liked to play games, so she thought she would wait until Yurri noticed she had put it on. He had probably already forgotten that he proposed to her with all the madness going on. In her mindset this signified that she had accepted it and him. She didn't know how long she would be able to play this little game of hers with him though. Janice was the type of girl to blurt out exciting news to a well-loved family member regardless of her hair color. With all the excitement going on Janice forgot that her god father, Dism Quantum, was on this planet right now looking for her.

While Yurri took his nap, the princess scoured through her purse for the small makeup kit and fold up mirror she had in there. She may have to be in the wilds right now, but she didn't have to look like she lived out here! She looked into her collapsible mirror and grimaced at what she saw. She looked bad. She had lines down her cheeks where her tears smeared some of her makeup. There was a bruise on her face where that brute had slapped her too. She had to fix that. Maybe she should switch to a water proof makeup. She always went shopping in areas where her girlfriends on this planet went but she never saw any water proof makeup at those places. Her friends here were still merely girls themselves planning and hatching ideas how to capture a proper man for themselves. They were fun to be around.

The princess worked on her makeup and hair while Yurri took his nap and Sixy went about depopulating this general area of local rodents and birds. He did have quite an appetite. She thought that her fault. She had only fed him a biscuit this morning while having breakfast. Sixy didn't seem to have much of an appetite then though. In reality she didn't know what type of diet he would need being that she never heard of an animal like Sixy before. She cheered him on while she fixed herself up. There were animals that would play, sing, and dance with you but generally those are more widely found in areas where more sentient people lived for some reason. Besides which she could never interfere with the natural order of things.

After finishing the last parts of her hair and face Yurri started rustling back into consciousness. She looked down on him with a smile. He was starting to gain a resistance to her kisses. With his first groans someone came out of the forest. It was that Jai with UP5! Janice stood up when she noticed them waving to them. What was that Jai's name again? She was never formally introduced to him when he pointed her in the right direction to find Yurri after those Enohps chased them.

"UP5 you found us!" she cried waving to them bouncing happily. UP5 came up to her and made some beeps and bops she didn't understand. "Oh, I'm sorry UP5," Janice said putting a hand to her mouth just remembering the state Décore was in right now. "Décore was put into stasis with my hair blond so I wouldn't be too much trouble for those bad men." Yurri, after coming to completely, stood up rubbing the back of his head.

It was then that Janice noticed the last person of the group that had found them. It was Ron! She jumped over the log and hid behind Yurri squealing. Sixy, sensing his mistress's distress, got in-between her and the new comers. The little ferret-like animal somehow became several times as large while its fangs and claws grew longer making him look much fiercer. All of the newcomers stopped and backed away from the ferocious looking nonlittle animal. Sixy's fur stood on end too. Janice obviously missed Yurri's mention of Ron.

"Whoa there missy it's just us," the Jai said with his hands up.

"Yeah but Ron is right behind you!" she said pointing at him. "He's the reason…"

Yurri was at her side getting her to lower her arm. "Yes, he's here happily helping us rescue you." He leaned in close and whispered something into Janice's ear.

"Oh!" Janice said putting her hand to her lips again. She waved at Sixy telling him to come over and picked him up. When the ferocious animal calmed down, he shrunk to his normal size, odd to say the least. "Ok Ron I'll let you in our group for now, but you should better be sure your hands are to your sides when you are behind me!" she said glaring at him. "I remember while we were dating that your hands had trouble wandering around and pinching." She gave him one more glare for good measure crossing her arms underneath her chest with Sixy around her neck.

"Oh, you don't have to worry about that anymore," Ron said a little drunkenly. He grabbed into one of his pockets and brought out a small circular holo-projector and turned it on smiling stupidly. "They say if I help you guys get out of here safely, I'll have a whole harem of beautiful alien women who won't mind me pinching them at all!" he said with a greedy look on his face staring while drooling a little at the holo-projected alien woman.

Yup that was the same old Ron she knew and... acknowledged that existed. She looked to her Jai boyfriend again. "Yurri what are we going to do now? Draxus never let's go of a hunt easily," she said frowning while grabbing and hugging Yurri's right arm. He squirmed a little, but she kept her hold on him.

"Ach," he said shaking his head and looked to the other Jai. "Hey Rialin, what do you think we should do now?"

"I doubt it very much we'll be able to get out of these woods without encountering Draxus and his gang again. We'll have to go north to the city, find your hover car again, and hope we find some police soon afterwards."

Yurri viewed them all and looked like he was measuring their worth. He shook his head looking grim. "While we make our way out of here, I think we should form a protective triangle around those of us who can't defend themselves," he said to Rialin looking at Janice and UP5.

"I can defend myself well enough!" Janice said urgently not wanting to be a burden on anyone. Her boyfriend looked at her shaking his head.

"I won't risk you getting hurt Jan," Yurri said looking down into her eyes while holding her shoulders. Ohh her boyfriend was so brave and chivalrous! But she could defend herself! She had training since she was a little girl to do just that.

"But I can defend myself!" she argued pounding his chest ineffectively pushing away from him. "Remember I've had training for this. You remember what I told and showed you this morning!" She looked down pouting.

"Yes, but you can only do those things when you can change your hair color. If we could find a way to unlock Décore for you to get to a proper hair color I would let you but that doesn't look like an option," he said while propping up her chin to look him in the eyes. Oh her boyfriend was so cool!

"I may be able to help you with that problem I think," a deep voice came from behind one of the nearest trees and out pops Professor Tom.

"BlaAahHhG!!!" Yurri screamed jumping and falling backward while flailing his arms. Well he lost the coolness that he was building up there pretty quickly. He must really be tense.

"Oop sorry about that but I couldn't help but overhear that you seem to be in quite the dire straits right now," Tom said looking embarrassed that he made Yurri flip out so.

"What are you doing here man?!" her boyfriend asked loudly while getting back on his feet. "Have you been stalking us this whole fricken' time since we left your lab yesterday?!" Yurri inquired, a bit aggravated, while Janice helped him get to his feet.

"Yes," the loony man said getting a wide range of surprised looks from everyone. "Jai Master Rialin I think it was a very good idea of you telling me to stay back just in case you needed my help." Tom looked to the Jai. Everyone regarded the Jai suspiciously.

"Whoa hey I told you to stay back at the city while I kept an eye on them! Not to follow us!" Rialin said waving one hand stressfully. So, the Jai had encountered the mad scientist while he had been following them too.

Yurri looked at Janice and quietly whispered to her, "Just how many people have been stalking us lately? Get a hobby people!" he finished that sounding very much like he wanted to sigh at that too. But, good for him, he held it back. Janice nodded her head in agreement to Yurri.

"So, wait," she said while walking up to Professor Tom. "You think you can unlock Décore? How did you know about her in the first place?"

The mad scientist gave her a wry grin. "You don't think I've learned a little something about you two while following you around?" Okay now she was sorry for asking.

"Alright," Yurri said since he saw that Tom was beginning to freak out Janice. "If you can help us with Janice's hair that'd be great but after we get that done, I'm not sure how we can protect you from the guys who're after us right now."

"Oh, you don't have to worry about me," Tom said as he motioned Janice to bend down for him after he came close enough. "You have experiment six six six with you and I'm also willing to loan you UP5 to help get you out of this too. This droid has a special mode where it becomes my bodyguard too." He pulled some tools out of one of his pockets and started tinkering with Décore on Janice's head. "And I may not look like it, but I am very good at avoiding attention." He continued talking about the surprising reactions coming from experiment 666. It was surprising for him that Janice was able to tame the little monster so. He mentioned that he should have probably thought it would have reacted better to someone with more estrogen in them anyways.

After tinkering around with Décore for a bit her little hair droid finally rebooted. "Ugh," Janice's little droid said. "What happened? Princess, are you alright?!"

Janice smiled as her well-loved little droid came back online and she patted her. "I'm alright for now Décore but we need to get going before those bad men find us again." The princess quickly explained what happened over the past couple of hours. "So, I need you to change my hair red, so I can figure out how to defend myself better and be a help to Yurri and everyone else."

Décore complied with Janice's request and once she was a redhead, she got a good idea. "You boys stay here while I go change. I can't fight in a skirt," Janice told them while putting her hair into a pony tail. "I'll only be gone for a minute or two." The more confident sounding and determined Janice left them into a denser part of the forest to go change into more suitable clothes taking her purse with her.

About fifteen minutes passed before Janice came back to them looking like she had spent an hour dressing and prepping. She now had on a red blue armored body suit that obviously had not been in closet of clothes she got from Tom. For the mad scientist was just as surprised as everyone else in this transformation of Princess Janice Agra. She didn't have her purse on her anymore too though she did have on a blue pack on her back. Her new clothes/armor had a dark gray vest that conformed to her feminine figure nicely with long gloved sleeves and wide lighter gray bracelets seemingly sown onto her wrists and ankles. The padding on her feet was black and in boot form that was just the right size for her even though they looked heavy and sturdy. She had done up her red hair into a bun that was on the nape of her neck tightly bound. This clothing was loose but not baggy and form fitting, mainly dark blue, and looked like it was comfortable on Janice. She still had Sixy around her neck.

"Professor Finny, you said that UP5 has another mode for combat?" She looked to the mad scientist and he nodded. "Please switch it to that mode for us now. I get the feeling that we've been waiting here for too long. Those men should be upon us any minute now."

Tom nodded his head and went to work fixing up UP5 for that. [Ugh,] the translation of UP5 from Décore sounded through Janice's skull into her ear drums. [I've always hated this,] it groaned. [The change is very uncomfortable, and this also messes with my personality profile too,] it said while Tom worked at some switches of its inner core.

While Tom did that Janice started informing the Jai Rialin, Yurri, and Ron on what they could expect from a fight with Draxus and his goonies. "Whelp that does it for UP5 now," the mad scientist said closing up UP5's circuit board. "I'll just go and find myself a nice place to hide while you people intermingle with those ruffians." He tipped his hat to them, which was kind of weird considering he didn't have one on and wished them good luck disappearing into the woods.

"Before we go," Janice said looking at Ron. "I have something I want to say to you Ron." She came up in front of him. Ron towered over her but that didn't stop her from flipping him over her shoulder. Ron grunted as he bounced off the ground a full three yards from where Janice threw him. A blaster he had on his person went off too but that was okay because it went off pointed at the ground. "That was for chasing me around the galaxy like you've been doing for the past couple of years," she said brushing off her hands. "And I don't want to find you doing it again or I am personally going to do some very unpleasant things to your reproductive organs myself!" she exclaimed mockingly repeating what Ron had yelled when they ran from him yesterday.

Ron groaned getting up. "If I had known about your special 'abilities' I'd never have bothered you in the first place," he grumbled to himself whipping out the small holo-projector Yurri gave him turning it on to view. Maybe he was reminding himself what the reward for going through with this was.

"Jai Master Epoch, can you remember where the hover car was parked?" Janice said getting down to business.

While the Jai was responding UP5 put something in first. [I don't think we need the hover car miss. If we're simply going to make a beeline to the police, I think it would be better if we headed straight that way through a construction zone.] Janice looked to the droid to consider what it was telling her. The useful droid pointed one of its tentacles a little bit to the north east of them. It was then that she noticed the droid fully. Its appearance had changed considerably somehow. It had all of its eight tentacle arms out right now looking thicker by some means. Its purple chassis had somehow gotten darker too. It now had two of its stalk "eyes" viewing her looking dangerous red instead of glowing docile white rimmed black. [That way is considerably shorter than going back to the hover car if we all ran. Is there a problem miss?] it asked in that deep man voice that Décore used to translate with. The droid had noticed a little surprise in Janice's face. Somehow Décore had made that voice tone sound more dangerous too. Tom must have made this droid in a very special way.

"Hey, are you listening to me?" Rialin tapped her shoulder.

"Oh sorry, UP5 was telling me something. So I tuned you out, sorry. Though I don't think we need to get back to the hover car anymore." Janice explained to everyone what UP5 had recently told her. "I think if we all ran the direction indicated by UP5 we'll come to the city faster than if we went back to the hover car."

"Sounds like a good idea," Rialin admitted. "Is everyone ready and able for a brisk run back into the city?" the Jai asked looking around at everyone.

"I think I can handle that," Yurri replied to the other Jai nodding.

"I have a jetpack so I might outrun you guys, so I think I'll stay in the back and take on anyone that tries to stop us," Ron said with a look of bloodlust in his eyes.

"You don't have to worry about me now," Janice said from behind Yurri right now. "I can take care of myself very well right now that I can remember a few talents and abilities that I have." Yurri jumped grabbing his toosh yelping. "And a few talents that I intend to show you later," she said grinning and winking at Yurri after pinching him. The young man's face flushed as he avoided his girlfriend's stare at him rubbing his bottom. UP5 gave that nodding gesture to the Jai to say that it was ready too.

"Alright let's go!" Janice cheered heartily while sprinting for the forest. As soon as she was in the forest proper a thin silver red line sprung from her left wrist band, latched onto a tall tree, sprung her into the air, and propelled her much faster than her companions on the ground with her suit enhancing her strength. She smiled as she swung tree to tree. Ever since her father first gave her this combat suit, she wanted to do this with it. The silver red lines retracted into her wrists when she needed them out of the way. She was now swinging high from the ground through the tall trees.

"Crap Jan where did you get something like that?"

Janice nearly fell to the ground when she heard her boyfriend's voice right next to her. She looked to her side and didn't see him at first but then he elevated into view. He and Rialin were doing that amazing Jai jump to keep up with her.

She looked at him impressed with the resourcefulness he used his Archai powers for. She kept swinging tree to tree, but everyone seemed to able to keep up with her well enough. Her suit was designed to give compressions to her body to maintain proper blood circulation regardless of what she was doing. With this blood compression going on she didn't have worry about all her blood going to her feet and passing out with all her swinging around. Ron was taking up the back while flying with his jetpack low and UP5 was hovering quickly between the two Jai and Ron.

Janice waited until she got the rhythm down where Yurri was face level to hear her before she spoke. "My father made this for me." She paused. "He worries about his children," another pause. "So he made me a purse that can convert into this special type of body armor," she blurted out quickly.

"Huh," he said while at her level again. "I'd hate to have to go up against... your father in battle... He sounds like a... fierce competitor." They chatted in this manner as they swung/leaped through the forest. They discussed the battle plan if Draxus ever caught up with them. They soon came to the construction site. It looked like they were reconstructing a whole section of the city here. The place looked deserted right now though. Janice could remember that the mayor of this city had announced not too long ago that they were going to make more residential areas for workers to move into all over the city. This planet was booming with business after all.

As soon as the forest stopped, they did too. There were halfway constructed buildings all over the place. They must still be a bit away from any populated area. There were abandoned construction vessels everywhere too. Maybe there was a holiday or something going on right now. The whole place was brick gray and steel blue with nothing living around at all. There were construction materials around everywhere along with a few random working droids meandering around the place also. They shouldn't have any communication problems now that they were in a more developed area.

"Does anyone have a communicator on them? Mine's probably back with our car after they stunned us." Janice said while making her way over a pile of construction rubble very unhappy she lost her phone. Yurri affirmed he had one and whipped it out. They all stopped when Yurri did.

"This can't be good," he said putting his communicator away. "I'm getting nothing but static. Draxus must be jamming us right now."

"Right you are," a voice came from behind one of the skeletal pillars of a halfway constructed building. Out came Draxus Lenox with smug smile on his face. "You didn't know I had eyes in the sky." He raised his arms and waved them making over a score or so men come out of their hiding places all heavily armed and armored. He then pointed his right arm out calling to someone and did the same on his left. Out came that monstrous droid fighting machine named X2-O0 with those horrible genetic pale-yellow creatures on their leashes looking eager. "Ever since your mother married your father and took over the throne, they have been making my life a nightmare," Draxus said like he was going to start a long exposition. "I worked hard my whole life in building up my status on planet Tyy since I got there years ago. While the Kaiser's empire was in power, I tried to lay low not wanting their attention. When the Kahn was finally overthrown, I thought my luck had changed at…" Draxus dived to the left when a support beam launched for his head.

"Yurri!" Janice exclaimed to her boyfriend who had swept his hand throwing out that beam using the Archai.

Yurri, embarrassed, shrugged sheepishly to his girlfriend. "I hate long pointless talks. Let's just get this over with," he said igniting his orange luminblade.

AN ORBITING DILEMMA

"Attack but have the Rem beasts capture the princess! They may maul her a bit, but the Rems should bring her to us alive. My pets do like to play with their victims quite a bit before..." Draxus shouted those orders to his men while grinning wickedly at Janice.

"Scatter!" Yurri yelled to everyone. "They'll have a harder time taking us all down if they can't gang up on us!"

The X2-O0 machine gave a gigantic leap towards them. They had all been scattering long before it launched itself, so it landed with a crash on none of them. UP5 took advantage of the monster machine's unbalanced posture and instigated an attack on the huge machine's joints launching itself at the monster. Somehow UP5's tentacles had changed into drills and hyper saws which it was attacking X2-O0 with. Ron had pulled his helmet mask from the nape of his neck entirely over his face looking like a ready eager grinning armored demon face, obviously designed to scare his prey. Rialin and Ron went after the various henchmen at either side where they were with demon Ron straightening his grenade belt and picking some out to start throwing smiling viciously through the terrifying sharpness shape of his helm. Yurri had his orange luminblade ignited by now and was deflecting blaster bolts as they came at him. Janice ran into the construction zone to draw their attention for she was the only one they were after. As she ran silver red liquid came from her collar rapidly enveloping her head giving her a see-through protective head visor helmet.

As soon as she reached one of those unfinished skeleton buildings, she flung out a red silver line to propel her up to it. When Janice was about fifteen floors up, she stopped and viewed the chaos that was going on down on the ground, but she found out she wasn't alone on that skeleton building. Those eight pale yellow monsters were climbing quickly up the skeleton structure.

Janice's face visor slid back. "Okay Sixy," the princess addressed her small companion that was still around her neck grabbing him giving her pet a kiss. "Sick um!" She flung her small ferocious pet with great aim at the nearest Rem beast below her. Sixy landed on the monster's face making it fall off the building after a ferocious attack. Sixy had grown dozens of times as large as his original form and looked almost akin to the Rem beasts though a different color, a longer snout, and longer legs. They fell off the building many flights to the ground. Janice knew that her pet would be alright though. She trusted in him. Her protective see-through part of her helmet slid back into place quickly as she readied herself.

The skeleton building shook when X2-O0 crashed into it. The monster droid grabbed hold of UP5 and tossed it high into the air. It then turned to look at where Janice was opening its compartments to launch much smaller saucer shaped dirty silver droids with five long tentacles coming from their undersides.

The princess didn't notice any of this though. She was too preoccupied by the Rem beasts to notice anything else. The level she was on right now was only six feet in width and felt flimsy being that it was made out of flat wooden boards. One of the abilities of this special suit on Janice was to spring forth a magnetic liquid that could solidify into any shape Janice could imagine, including short ranged weapons.

One of the much faster Rem beasts got to the level she was on and started stalking toward her quickly. She launched the first attack. Janice swung out her arm in a wide arc with a whip-like weapon with a small pointed mace at the end of it. After seven quick flicks of her right arm the beast, with many tears in its face with one of its eyes completely destroyed, forgot finesse and launched itself at the princess howling. Janice jumped off the side of the board walk only getting a hit on her right hip, that would bruise badly, but mainly dodged the worse of the attack. From her gray wrist bands launched that special liquid that latched onto the railing. Janice did a wonderful dive then swung up around and over onto the opposite side and used her momentum to kick off the Rem beast over the edge. She wasn't able to get her footing afterwards though for one of those small robots that the X2-O0 launched grabbed her left wrist with one of its five tentacles. After wrenching herself away painfully, popping her hand out of joint, she swung a whip mace from her right wrist entangling it around all five of the droid's arms. Janice did a wonderful flip somersault kick on top of the droid. The sharp jagged point she made come from the back of her left heel penetrated the saucer droid's exoskeleton making it land with a sparking crash on the walkway.

Janice got back to her feet quickly trying to take in her area. While quickly adjusting her popped out hand her suit covered it with red silver injecting a numbing healing agent in, made specifically for her physiology, while putting pressure on her damaged left wrist. Probably would have torn her hand off if not for her armor. She saw that underneath her those saucer droids and Rem beasts were fighting each other. These beasts and droids weren't very well organized. This was the only reason she hadn't been overwhelmed by now she realized. Someone on top of the X2-O0 machine was shouting at the below combatants. X2-O0 started shaking the frame of the skeleton building Janice was on now.

The princess threw out a silver red line to connect the next building over. Once the combatants organized themselves underneath her, she would be in trouble. She jumped off the skeleton building to swing to the next one over. In midflight her line was cut by an accidental, or not so accidental, blaster shot. It wasn't a clean cut for the special and armored way this liquid metal was made. The blast actually made her metal line turn into a sharp point before the laser cut it. When her line viciously snapped it threw her through the air spinning violently. She screamed as she plummeted the fifteen flights to the ground spiraling wildly. She was going to die and there was nothing she could do about that; she couldn't orient herself to get another line out in time.

She was only about a yard from the ground when she suddenly stopped in place in the air. She breathed hard with her brow dripping sweat as she looked to her right and saw Yurri with his hand out. He smiled in relief that he caught her in time. That relief was short lived. Draxus got a solid kick into Yurri's chest knocking him back a couple yards. "Get to higher ground! We'll hold them here!" Rialin, who was at Yurri's side helping him back up, shouted to her. The Jai used his blue orbs to keep Draxus and his goonies at bay as he helped her boyfriend.

Luckily for Janice she had already gotten her footing by the time Draxus had slam kicked her boyfriend. She was torn between helping the man whom she found she loved and heeding the Jai's very sound advice. She only stood in place for a few heart beats before something jumped on her making her stumble. It was Sixy! A much heavier and bigger Sixy but still it was her Sixy! Her pet must have landed on that Rem beast. He shrunk down to his normal size and wrapped himself around her neck hissing possessively at her. Janice wisely retreated running toward the nearest incomplete building to get up on with her fierce pet around her neck.

Those Rem beasts had disengaged their fight with those saucer droids which were fighting off a now recovered, though slightly dented, UP5 from their base droid X2-O0. As UP5 tussled with one of those saucer bots the fierce loyal droid tore it apart limb from limb with hyper saws and its drills spectacularly. Ron was facing off with two other men equipped with jet packs and full body armor too. They must be a couple of Draxus' lieutenants, his "eyes in the sky". There were dark blaster marks etched all over the bounty hunter's armor by this time with his helmet still making that evil vicious smile. He whipped out a grenade he had on him and threw it into where the lesser henchmen were taking cover to shoot at them. About a dozen henchmen threw themselves out from behind the cover when the grenade went off. Three of the henchmen that weren't fast enough flew into the air looking very badly burned and not quite whole.

Janice launched a silver red rope from her right wrist to get up one level on the nearest skeletal building. The six Rem beasts that were left followed the princess up onto that building, their claws raking deep gashes in the metal construction girders. Janice ran to the other side of the building with a plan of retaliation already in mind. She stopped at the edge of this level, turned around, and waited for the Rem beasts to all get up on this level. Once all the monsters were on the same girder running full on to get to her the princess launched herself over the edge viciously swinging around in a wide silver red arc to land a full-bodied kick into the Rem beast that was at the end of the others. Janice let her line retract and fell with the beast down to the ground. The young woman impaled the monster as she landed on it with a spike coming from her feet.

"Whoo!" she screamed in triumph while getting off the now dead impaled through the neck beast. The silver red metallic liquid spike retracted back into her boots as she secured her footing off the Rem. As she stood there the five remaining Rem beasts jumped down to ground level and warily started coming up to her. The odds were more even now. Sixy jumped off his mistress and grew in size again putting himself in-between the monsters and his mistress. Janice threw her hand up and something sparkled from her hand. Janice's silver red vibrating shuriken severed a rope that was holding building supplies high up. A couple tons of rubble fell and buried one of those Rem beasts killing it while the others barely escaped that. The princess had seen a pile of precariously perched building materials tied up there and had noted that.

With the odds even better matched the princess formed her weapons of choice from the silver red metallic liquid coming from her suit. She formed that spiked ball whip again in her numbed wrapped but still working left hand with a short-curved saber in her right. Sixy hissed fiercely as the remaining four monsters warily stalked in with him now a bit bigger than even them. They growled a deep guttural sound that chilled Janice's skin. This wasn't going to be easy. The beasts would be exceptionally more careful with her now.

Further off to the left of the princess UP5 was furiously fighting off seven of those saucer droids while at the same time trying to work its way into an area on the back of X2-O0 where it detected this monster machine's power source. X2-O0 couldn't reach the daring droid on its back with its four arms. The monstrous machine tried a different tactic to rid itself of the bothersome droid. It turned its back to one of the heavily constructed building frames and slammed its back into it. It did this a couple times until it was satisfied that it had crushed its assailant.

The resourceful and tricky UP5 had actually been planning for this. The X2-O0 machine had inadvertently smashed three of its own drones. UP5 had sent a signal of defense to the now hibernating and simple programmed construction droids that the clever droid had detected were here earlier. With these simple construction droids, it was easy to send out an all-around alert to any of these droids to defend their construction yard. Once a few of those construction droids woke up and after some quick hacking, with those construction droids open and alert for commands

UP5 gained full control over the simple robots. The jarring into the building had also automatically alerted these bots.

These bots were mainly built for construction projects so UP5 didn't expect them to last too long against a war machine like this. Maybe they would take down a couple of those bothersome saucer droids in the process. The resourceful droid only needed them to distract the monster machine long enough to get it under a construction site that it noticed wasn't entirely stable and would likely fall easily if anything jarred it strongly enough. UP5 only needed to get X2-O0 in the proper spot.

Yurri's chest hurt from where he had been kicked. He thought he had a few broken ribs. The Jai Rialin and Ron were doing a pretty good job at keeping the lesser henchmen at bay though neither of them looked like they could keep that up for very much longer. The young man turned Jai was trying his best to keep Draxus and his flying lieutenants away from Janice. She looked like she had her hands full on fighting off those Rem beasts that were left. It wasn't his choice to be the main opponent to the gang leader though. It just seemed to happen that way.

The young man flipped away when one of those flying men suddenly shot a blue foaming liquid from a rifle. He didn't think he could stop something like that with his luminblade. Yurri led these men away from where the main fighting was taking place hoping to disperse their strength they had in numbers. The three men after him right now had switched out their weapons to tube rifles that shot this foaming blue liquid. It sizzled on any area it landed and shortly made a depression on anything it was on. Draxus chuckled whenever the young man had to launch himself out of the way of the blue acid. This man was obviously proud of himself for coming up with a weapon that he could fight any menacing Jai with and get on even terms with them.

To counter the gangsters' attacks Yurri jumped up high onto one of those skeleton buildings. With a short reprieve in the fighting Yurri took in his current situation. Ron and Rialin were being sorely pressed by Draxus's henchmen seeing that those henchmen had somehow obtained acid rifles for themselves. UP5 was playing around with X2-O0 trying to taunt the giant into following it under one of the incomplete buildings using a couple construction droids that were somehow under UP5's control too. Janice was the one that looked the worst. She had a line of red liquid coming from her left shoulder that the young man hoped wasn't blood. Sixy was in a full-on brawl barely holding his own with one of those Rem beasts looking nothing but fur, fangs, and claws in a tornado.

This reprieve didn't last long for the young man though. The three jet packed men flew up to his level quickly enough. They continued shooting that blue acid at him but Yurri retaliated with an attack of his own. He grabbed a construction chain with the Archai cutting it off with his luminblade and threw it spinning at the gangsters. It only connected with one of Draxus's henchmen spinning him for a loop out of control hopefully putting this man out of the fight. The young man dropped to ground level again furiously searching for things to fling at the gangsters. After finding one metallic support beam in a pile of rubble he levitated it in the air spinning towards his nearest enemy. Being the not so good aim that he was that beam only clipped the flying gangster's feet spinning him out of control.

As the young man watched the gangster bounce on the ground he wondered where the boss gangster was. A tremendous pain erupted from Yurri's back flinging him to his chest sliding a couple yards in the grainy dirt. Adrenalin running through his veins the young man dizzily turned over to see what struck him. Draxus was flying there a little above with his left foot in the air. The evil man grinned wickedly as he let blue acid come out of his rifle pointed at Yurri.

Janice bit back pain as she caught her footing from a recent backflip jump, one of the Rem beasts recently died by her hand with a saber through the eye. But that kill had come at a cost. Another one of the Rem beasts got a pretty good slash on her thigh because she chanced getting that kill. She already had a slash on the back of her left shoulder. Her armor should have protected her from that, but she also noticed these monsters making big gashes in solid rock and metal. She suspected she dodged the worse those Rem beasts could afflict from a blow like that because of her fine armor. Sixy was still in a fury fight with another one of those monsters not too far away. The last two were organizing their attacks more coordinated as this fight went on. Janice suspected these beasts to be semi-sentient like she suspected of Sixy.

To buy her more time she took advantage of a skill she had learned from one of her many dancing classes as a child. She spun with her arms out shortening the lengths of her mace ended whips initially then lengthened them as she gained momentum. She landed about a dozen good hits on those monsters forcing them to back off with many open wounds on their faces and bodies. She only stopped when she noticed her whips not making contact anymore. She stopped her fierce pirouette facing the direction of the Rems with her arms in front of her in a defensive position. The two monsters stayed away from her sizing her up giving the young woman a few precious seconds of reprieve. All of a sudden something was on her back clawing its way up to her neck. The princess irrationally shrieked panicked grabbing at her back forgetting all the years and hard work of her self-defense training. The Rem beasts thankfully didn't know how to take advantage of the fierce scream distraction their prey momentarily had.

Janice quickly calmed herself down grabbing at whatever it was on her back. She grabbed something furry that somehow felt familiar. The princess brought the offending creature in front of her and saw that it was Sixy! So that was why her survival instincts hadn't kicked off. Sixy was no threat to her! Apparently, he had finished off that other beast he was fighting. The young woman, a lot calmer now, smiled as she placed a very ruffled up and battered looking Sixy in front of her. It was still going be a hard fight but now the young woman believed they would win it shortly.

So here was Yurri, lying on the ground, with a deadly stream of corrosive deadly acid coming towards his face in a deadly way. One of things that this young man didn't know about wielding the Archai was that certain talents that any individual Jai had could vary greatly. Such as certain Jai couldn't levitate anything at all unless they touched said object first. While a few others found it easier to move nonsolid things like gases and liquids. Luckily for Yurri he was one of the latter.

As that stream of deadly acid came toward Yurri's face he reflexively flung out one of his hands and diverted the stream to harmlessly sizzle off to his right. Draxus hovered there for a second confused at what happened. Jai weren't supposed to be able to do that. Thank goodness for the young man that the gangster didn't know about this ability either.

Draxus continued to fire mercilessly on the young man turned Jai but with each shot Yurri gained in confidence easily getting the hang of diverting the liquid flows of blue acid. Yurri got his footing again while still diverting the acid off to his side. Seeing that this wasn't working anymore Draxus tried a new tactic. He pulled out one of his short-fused grenades and threw it at the young man turned Jai. Yurri had to cartwheel himself out the way of the explosion. Though when he did that, he could not help but place his hands into one of the puddles of acid. The force of the blast threw the poor lad head over heels away from Draxus.

When Yurri landed on his back with his hands up in front of his face he bit back a scream of pain while instinctively dissipating the acid from his hands using the Archai. Oh, they burned… There go his finger prints. One of Draxus's lieutenants had recovered himself by this time and was honorably shooting at Yurri while he was on the ground with some more acid. The young man flipped himself back onto his feet, his luminblade still on in his right hand and thankfully unaffected by the acid he had removed it so quickly. He made the acid intended to hit him veer around in a loop and hit that henchman in the face. The henchman fell to the ground screaming as he clawed at his ruined face.

As Yurri and Draxus took a breath glaring at each other a heavy empty construction bag dropped from its perch higher up from one the incomplete buildings landing nearby Yurri. The gangster took the initiative and lobbed a special type of grenade at the young man. The grenade only made it halfway before it broke into smaller cluster grenades that shot forward even faster than the parent grenade. Yurri desperately threw himself out of the way rolling, inadvertently touching that construction bag, but his right leg got blasted by a few of those smaller cluster grenades. The young man struggled to catch his balance from that roll his leg bleeding badly. As Draxus dug for another grenade to throw. Yurri painfully kicked that construction bag with his wounded leg at the mobster. As Draxus threw his grenade the construction bag enveloped his hand. Yurri had guided that bag using the Archai. What had been Draxus Lenox was obliterated by his own highly explosive grenade weapon.

The young man, exhausted from this fight, and the adrenalin in his blood depleted, painfully fell to his knees not seeing any more threats. His hands still burned, and he would need to get them looked at. They hurt so much he stuffed them under his armpits. Suddenly, an entire skeleton building collapsed to Yurri's left. The young man's mind was feeling numb from the intense fight, so he merely stared blankly at it as the building collapsed crushing X2-O0 underneath it.

"Yurri are you sure you're all right?" Janice asked her boyfriend for like the hundredth time after everything had finally calmed down. Her specially made suit/purse had soaked back up her helmet visor so her face was fully showing again.
"Yeah I'm okay Jan, but I think you need to see a medic about your side and shoulder," Yurri said trying to get his girlfriend off him and stop worrying about him. He was sitting uncomfortably on a pile of construction rubble with many policemen widespread out in the area now with his leg and hands roughly bandaged by Janice along with some low quality pain healing cream she had on her too. The surviving henchmen had all been taken and put under arrest by this time. There were teams of crime scene investigators all over this place.
The police had noticed all the commotion going on in this construction area and had come to investigate. The Jai Rialin flashed a badge —*Now where did he get that? Yurri didn't know Jai even had badges.*— to the local police and filled them in on everything that happened to them. The police called in some help making sure to get medics and med bots down here too. Ron was off with some other policemen trying to see if he could get a bounty reward for being a part of the group of people that took out such a violent criminal.
"I'm alright sweetie. See?" Janice lifted her arm to show her damaged side. The silver red liquid that came from her

suit had bandaged her cuts. She even still had her left wrist wrapped, compression wise, with some red silver liquid too. "This suit can also do minor surgery tasks on my body too when I'm not jumping around too much that is. My Daddy thought of everything when he built and designed these suits for me and my siblings." Janice had changed her hair back to a blond color after it was declared all was safe. "And don't worry about any damages done here today Yurri. My special princess insurance should easily be able to cover all damage costs. Even a collapsed building!" She smiled smugly at him. Why did it sound like she had to rely on this "princess insurance" more than once?

 The young man tried a couple more times to get away from Janice, but she clung almost fiercely to one of his less damaged arms protesting that he should rest. He sighed knowing this to bug her, but she didn't seem to notice. The Jai Rialin came up to them after talking to some police men giving them some orders on what to inspect and do. He bowed to Janice politely calling her by her full real name and asked if he could borrow Yurri for a moment alone.

 Janice bit her lip not looking like she was about to give up Yurri, but the young man gently touched her shoulder and gave her a serious look. She tugged on her pony tail, she had let her hair down when all was declared calm also, not looking happy but gave into the Jai and stepped away from them out of hearing distance going over to UP5 to check on the dutiful droid with her pet around her neck again. As soon as she was besides the helpful droid and talking to it UP5 reached into one of its compartments and brought out her mobile phone giving it back to her. Janice jumped and hugged, kissing the diligent lovable droid right on one of its eyestalks making all its visible appendages straighten and quiver violently.

After looking at that silly scene with Janice and UP5 the Jai shook his head bemused and started talking to Yurri. "Jai are few and far in-between with the talents and strength you have my friend. I am very sure you would receive an honorable position if you committed yourself to train to become a full Jai."

"I'm not sure if that is for me Rialin," Yurri said while shaking his head. "The only reason I survived and was able to help this day is because of all the talents and abilities you gave me. I can think of a hundred times where I should have died if it wasn't for what you gave me." Yurri shrugged wincing a little at the pain in his ribs.

Rialin frowned furrowing his brow looking down on the young man. "So, you think that any man that can pick up a blaster and fire it is automatically a qualified soldier?"

Where did that obscure question come from? The young man looked down thinking on that question. "No, not everyone who can pick up a blaster can automatically become a soldier. It takes determination, skill, training, and wit to make a competent soldier."

"All of these, minus some of the abilities you got from me, were exhibited by you while we went to rescue your girlfriend. Once you got into it you were the one giving out the orders. Not me. You stepped into the role of a leader so naturally I was surprised to know that you had never done anything like it before," the Jai said viewing him up and down. "You seem to have more natural talent than you give yourself credit for. This is an open invitation for you if you ever want to explore your full abilities with the Archai." The Jai gave him a formal half bow, then handed him his contact information. "I'll only be here for about a week to fill out paper work," he grimaced. "I need to get back to my family, but if there is anything you need to talk to me about you have my contact information." Rialin went off to talk to the police chief again.

Yurri sat there shaking his head pocketing Rialin's contact card. This was all way too much for the poor fellow to take in. His entire universe had been flipped completely upside down starting only yesterday. He thought he liked Janice, but he didn't know if he loved her. And she was royalty too for crying out loud! One day she would likely become a queen or something similar to that. He knew that he couldn't handle all the political implications that he would be brought to bear if he continued dating her. Let alone if she ever wanted to marry him! Their relationship could never last the test of time.

He came to the decision that it was pointless to stall the inevitable any more. He only stalled that first time because he thought it would be difficult and very emotional to break up with her as a blond. And then things got even more complicated. No point in trying to dodge this anymore.

"Janice!" Yurri called out. A new group of people had arrived by this time looking like they were the medics and various other groups of people too. Maybe these were sent to help the CSI men. Janice looked at him and started to come over to him patting UP5's damaged exoskeleton. Once she was close enough, he took in a deep breath and started talking. "Janice there is something very serious that I need to discuss with you. After these past few days I need to let you know where I stand on a couple things." She nodded her head still coming up to him not looking like she totally understood where this solemn tone in his voice came from. "This has to do with our relationship. Jan I—"

He couldn't finish for Janice was squealing in delight while hopping all of a sudden. "Uncle Dism?! Is that you?!" She cried happily clapping her hands and ran to whatever it was that caught her attention. She ran over to an older looking man that looked like he was in charge of a group of men that were carrying some equipment. One of the medics, dressed in white, came over to look at Yurri. It was an older but still pretty woman with a couple lines in her face with jet black hair, looked like she dyed it though.

As the nurse checked his ribs, hands, and legs touching them lightly and waving some scanning instruments over him and asking him some questions too about what he went through. The young man sighed in resignation again. This was only a short reprieve of what must be done. Janice sure was happy to see that man. She almost knocked the older man over when she gave him a lunging hug. She excitedly started talking to this fellow barraging him with things Yurri couldn't hear they were so far away.

"This might sting a little at first, but it should start alleviating the pain much more in your hands and leg," the nurse said as she applied a stinging balm to Yurri's poor blistered hands and wounded leg after gently removing his make shift bandages. She asked him to remove his shirt, so she could inspect his chest more thoroughly. He did so, with her gentle help, and saw that a big boot print was in the left side of his chest. The nurse confirmed her suspicions about him having some broken ribs, so she gave him a liquid to drink and said she'd be right back telling him to drink it all by that time. She needed to get some special bandages and supplies for him.

Yurri drank the oily bitter tasting liquid stoically. As he did the pain started subsiding slowly but reliably. This was supposed to be Kagna-Aid. Not very much unlike the Kagna fluid doctors bodily put their patients into to help with the healing process. Though, of course, this wasn't as effective as the full body dipping. It would accelerate the healing in his body but not at the rate of full body dip would. All that Yurri knew about this particular type of liquid was that it was made by purple slug-like aliens who guarded the secret of this quite fiercely and that it was a special type of bacteria or virus.

Janice with the old man, he looked familiar somehow, he had on ranch cloths, came skipping up to Yurri looking very happy. "Yurri, honey, this is my Uncle Dism Quantum! I knew I should have recognized that type of build that mansion we were at yesterday had." She giggled giddily. What was she so happy about? Well at least he knew where this guy came from. Yurri recognized him now. "I told him all about us and everything we've gone through. I even told him that you proposed to me with a wonderfully beautiful ring too!" She flashed around a ring she had on her left hand for everyone to see. "I hope you don't mind but I asked Uncle Dism if he would make all the preparations for our wedding and honeymoon. I know your mom would probably want in on this too so later I'll contact her myself and tell her what's up! Speaking of moms…" Janice put a finger to her full lips. "I need to get a hold of my mother and fill her in! I don't know how she'll take all of this mind you being that I haven't seen anyone of my family members for a couple years now. Ohh but she'll be so proud and happy to hear that I'm hooked up with the man that took down Draxus Lenox, scourge of my home planet!" She bounced again in a way that was quite pleasant. She looked at her god-father again, "Uncle Dism would you please look after Yurri for me while I find a way to contact Daddy and Mom?" The much older man nodded his head while the princess kissed his cheek and went away to find a decent communicator for her to contact her parents with.

The older man, Dism, looked down on the sitting younger man and caught him by the shoulder. Yurri nearly fell completely over. "What the frell? What the fretch? What the frack? What the Flipping Frelling Fracking Fretching CRAP DOG JUST HAPPENED!!??" the young man exclaimed turning exceptionally white shaking his head.

"A word of advice to you my young friend, you might want to clean up your language around my godchild Janiece. She doesn't take too kindly to filthy language," Dism cautioned Yurri.

"What the frelling crap just happened?!" the young man exclaimed again. "Just a minute ago I was gearing myself to break up with her, but now I'm *engaged!?*" the frightened and bewildered young man cried out loud.

Dism chuckled a little bit with his hands over his belly. "You seem to be as confused as I am in this particular situation. I truly enjoy the fact that my godchild found someone she likes enough to marry but I'm still wondering how the wedding ring she has is the exact match to the one I had in display back in the room I left you in to wait." The old farmer tapped his chin thoughtfully giving Yurri a scrutinizing look.

Oop, the young man remembered now. That weird reaction Janice had when they met up in the farming mansion was her thinking that he had just proposed to her. He had totally forgotten about that ring he was looking at, that he shouldn't have been, back at Dism's place. "Uhh, I think I know how sir," Yurri said shakily raising one hand carefully. "I was looking at that particular ring, like you told me not to, when this weird rodent droid attacked my face. Sorry, but while I had that thing on my face, I… might have broken a couple rare, invaluable, and irreplaceable items, sorry." Yurri cringed a bit expecting an explosion of anger from the old man.

To his surprise Dism only chuckled waving his hand. "Oh, they're just things, and not even the originals! Those particular security droids were picked out by my oldest daughter. She has a fetish in liking rodents so to placate her I took a few security ones to roam around the mansion where ever I'm at," he waved a hand shaking his head while smiling. "I asked an old friend of mine, who is the curator from an old museum of varieties of antiquities, if I could borrow some of his material to showcase them to the entire city for free. Instead of giving me the originals he gave me ones he had made by a spectacular artist and his droid helpers. Magnificent work really. My friend is quite picky about his relics. He had his originals packed away while I had his decoys. This was a ploy to draw Janiece out of hiding mind you. She does have a sharp eye for antiquities like that. And I was hoping to draw her out into the open there."

Yeah that was right. Janice had hinted to him earlier this week, quite blatantly, to take her to an art exhibit that was to open up in about a week or two. At first, he was a bit hesitant but when she mentioned that it was free, she hooked him. Maybe that was why the plan Draxus had seemed so rushed.

The young man continued to explain that because he was closely looking at that ring at that time and how he got attacked by that little droid he somehow got into the kneeling position with the ring out in front of him as Janice entered the room.

"Ha, that sounds like luck to me for you my boy," Dism chuckled. "The only item with any real or substantial value was that ring. I had that ring made for my godchild's birthday the year she disappeared. And besides which I truly believe you can make her happy." Yurri gave the older man a very doubtful look and he chuckled jollily again. "Did you know that she never by choice allows her hair to be blond? One of the main reasons it took so long to find her here. I can tell you that before she vehemently hated being a blond. She thought it made her stupid." Yurri nodded to that. "But I can also tell she maintains that look right now for you. She wants to make you feel comfortable around her."

Yurri shifted uncomfortably at that on the pile of construction rubble he was sitting on and the luminblade he had on his knees fell off. He reflexively started to bend down to pick it up again, but he bent wrong and grabbed his chest coughing painfully. Dism politely picked up the luminblade and placed it back on Yurri's lap. "You may keep that weapon if you want to. An old Jai friend gave me his old blade to thank me for helping rebuild his destroyed house after an attempt at his life and family." The old farmer shook his head musing. "The Jai these days sure have rough and hectic lives. And please do not worry about all the broken items. I have many truckloads of copies hidden away just in case. Don't want to cancel any pleasant school trips now." He patted Yurri's shoulder lightly and went off to attend to some other duties leaving Yurri alone again.

That old nurse came back with some bandages for Yurri but lightly scolded him for not finishing his Kagna-aid. She had Yurri raise his arms and wrapped his chest applying some more healing ointment. But when she was done, she quickly stabbed him in the back with a needle in an embarrassing place. "Owww!" Yurri complained rubbing his recently injured area after the needle was withdrawn.

"That was for not finishing drinking what I gave you," she said in a grandmotherly tone. "That was an injection full of Kagna fluids. Since you didn't finish off drinking the Kagna-aid I thought you should have that. That also had some purification medicine in it because that acid was a type of poison too." She shook a finger at him. "I also have some gel that will turn your skin and hair back to their normal color if you want." Yurri gave her a puzzled look and she chuckled. "My grandchildren love to dress themselves up as aliens. They say it's a fashion statement." She chuckled again as she handed him a familiar looking bottle to get rid of the skin dye.

It had been about a week and a couple days since all the crazy incidents happened and right now Yurri was with his fiancée, Princess Janiece Agra, up on the exact same hill where all this started having a brunch date with her again. This past week had been so busy they had barely gotten the chance to even see each other. Janice had been so upset about that she grabbed Yurri when he was talking to his former boss and whisked him away back to where all the madness began to complete their interrupted brunch date.

They were back up on that familiar hill again, but with a lot of more stylish picnic accessories. Janice had UP5 come with them too to carry a collapsible table and various other picnicking necessities with it. Apparently, the princess had gotten such a liking of the dutiful droid she bought it from the mad scientist Tom. Tom consulted this with the droid he built and UP5 had come to a liking of Janice too. Also, Tom threw in giving the princess Sixy too as a wedding gift.

Yurri was dressed in the same fashion as he was in when they first attempted this date to Janiece's minor chagrin. Only the colors were different on his clothes. Brown on bottom, serviceable black on top. Looks like Yurri tries to be practical in all that he does, with, of course, his luminblade hooked his belt now too. Janice on the other hand was dressed in a one-piece knee length skirt that was vibrantly blue at the bottom with colorful light blue yellow swirls ascending up and over her shoulders. Her hair color was set to a greenish blond today also. Over the past few days she had been experimenting with what different odd hair colors did to her and this one made her find everything delightful making her laugh easily. After all was set up properly the two sat down for a word of grace.

After saying grace over the food Janice almost went into a hysterical fit of laughter. Yurri looked at his fiancée patiently waiting for her to tell him the punch line. "Oohhh..." said Janice catching her breath with one hand on her chest while the other fanned her face with her face a little red. "Before coming to get you for our date I was talking to my Mom. She told me the only reason why she tried to set me up with that old codger before was to trick and encourage me to find a man myself." She shrugged while perusing what was on their picnic table to eat. She giggled again. "So, if my Mom never thought to 'encourage' me we never would have found each other!" she said as she was deciding on what to eat first. "Looks like her plan worked! In a way. I didn't date anyone much before I went into hiding. I think that was because of everyone knowing my position," she speculated. "Too afraid to approach me. That and I trounced all my sparring partners... This wasn't the case though when I was in hiding. I was just another pretty face." She decided on a morsel and grabbed it.

Yurri only shook his head blandly. Of course, all this madness happened to him out of a misunderstanding between a parent and child. Oh well…

"So dear, when do you think you'll lose those Jai powers now?" she asked delicately nibbling on a well-made buttered croissant. Yurri had to have Rialin help him tell Janice that his current talent with the Archai wasn't permanent. He made sure to have her hair a brunet when it was explained to her too. She said that certain things made a lot more sense to her now that she knew the full story.

"In about a week or two I believe. Rialin gave me some meds he says I should take when the headaches start happening." Yurri cut into some bread putting some butter on the slab he took off it. "He says that the meds will mainly put me under until the headaches pass so I won't be much fun to be around then." He took a bite out of his buttered bread. After having a long talk with his parents Yurri had grudgingly come to an acceptance of his situation, might as well look on the bright side. Like, who in their right minds would not love to be married to a curvy beautiful smart girl like Janice?

"How is that Jai? I heard that his wife came here with all their children not too long ago." she said while feeding

Sixy a slab of meat. Well it was more like a barbequed full huge rodent but the little monster bit into it eagerly chewing threw bone.

Yes, Rialin's family came here to see him. After having their child his wife had packed up her children and started following her husband unbeknownst to him. To Rialin's great frustration! She was a very well-off business woman with a strong perspective set on her family. Yurri told what he knew about the Jai while wiping his face with a napkin.

"Oh!" Janice said remembering something abruptly putting her food down. "Just to let you know I checked up on what happened to all the people that were in that horrible traffic accident we saw. Blessedly there were no fatalities or permanent injuries. Modern day safety suspension hover car straps saves the day again!" she said to Yurri with a thankful smile on her face. "And just because they happen to be in the way of mobsters trying to get at us, I paid off all their medical bills and even helped them all purchase new vehicles too! They all were certainly thankful and more than happy that I did that for them!" She smiled fulfilled by the good deed she'd done. Yurri nodded to his betrothed smiling also as he bit into his meat and gravy filled roll.

"Whatever happened to your old boyfriend, Ron? Haven't seen him since the day we fought off Draxus and his goonies," Yurri asked looking at Janice with his food zeroed in on impact to his mouth.

"Oh Ron," she said frowning remembering about her old bounty hunter boyfriend. "Oddly enough I saw him when I went to check in on Professor Tom about the things I would need to know about taking care of Sixy." Janice ruffled her nose in a cute way showing displeasure as she pulled her blond green hair behind an ear. "Ron had tried out that cologne you gave him afterwards and apparently he got really good results from it. He was talking to Mr. Finny about how he could get more of the stuff." Janice dabbled with her food looking for something in particular to eat. "They came to an agreement in short order," she said stabbing a piece of food bringing it into her mouth. She chewed and swallowed her food before speaking again. "Where Ron becomes Mr. Finny's lab rat in exchange for some pay and an unlimited amount of that particular type of cologne. Though I do think something very funny came from this." The young man quirked his head with a question on his face and Janice lightly giggled more than happily at him. "Ron has a thirty-five-year-old female manager who's also his older sister that wasn't too happy to hear that Ron quit the bounty hunting business. Thus she came over to have a talk with his new employer. To make a long story short she found out Mr. Finny to be a lonely but very rich scientist. Poor Mr. Tom never knew what hit him." She giggled a bit louder in her hand this time. "I talked to that woman and she plans on forcing him to ask her to marry him within a month. Poor Tom," she said while wiping her face with a napkin. "Apparently she has mutant feet with two big toes on each foot on either side. Tom won't stand a ghost of chance against her once she flashes him with those!" She winked at Yurri giggling at the silliness of it all.

"So, when do you think you'll sign up and go to Xevim 3 to start your Jai training?" Janice asked while quirking him a wicked grin. "You know I might just try and see if I'm not Archai sensitive myself. I think that would be fun!"

Yurri's attention wasn't on Janice though. He was viewing something extremely strange right now. A man with a blond woman in his arms dressed as a bride quickly ran around the bend of the next hill over into view. He looked really panicked stricken running with that woman in his arms. Yurri stood up wondering if he should offer this man any help. The next thing that happened made the young man's jaw drop. A mob of a mixture of humans and aliens ran around the bend screaming angrily obviously intending to do that poor man some harm.

"Hey Jan, I think you're going to have to excuse me for a moment. But please get our hover car up and running. I'm going to see if I can't help that guy and girl," he said while still looking at the madness down below.

"Ok honey," she said. Yurri looked at her and was a little surprised. She had somehow quickly changed into her body armor with her hair red. She kissed his cheek and went about getting things set up with help from UP5. As Yurri readied himself to jump into action he wondered what this poor fellow's story was. That is when the TW4 came rumbling out of the forest snapping trees and joining the pursuit pointing its blasters at the unfortunate couple. "Aww come OONNN!!!"

About the Author from the Author

Okay so since I am not nearly as good as telling stories about myself as I am about the stories I imagine up I asked my dear sisters to write a short diddy for me better explaining what I've lived through. The short of this is I've lived through a car wreck, got all four limbs shattered like glass with the car on top of me snapping my femurs and massive brain trauma to boot which, more or less, crippled my left leg and hindered left side movement a bit. Elegant words about the event I know. I'm getting better tho! A walker is an upgrade from a wheelchair I promise! But please enjoy my sisters' more eloquent description of my situation!

About the Author from his dear sisters

Human resilience in the face of insurmountable odds. Faced with debilitating injuries, both of the body and the brain, Brett Wortham overcame the odds to walk, conversate and tell his stories once more. He has always been a storyteller. His mind is full of fantastical, witty, entertaining tales woven together with his own unique touch. Though a car accident took many memories and ease of movement, his brain remained awash in stories and creative expression.

He finds joy in sharing with the world this universe that he has created. Through stories like An Orbiting Dilemma and Lost Heart of the Magoce he reaches out to leave his own legacy on the world and touch the hearts and minds of others.

www.ingramcontent.com/pod-product-compliance
Ingram Content Group UK Ltd.
Pitfield, Milton Keynes, MK11 3LW, UK
UKHW022214230426
12048UKWH00016BA/845